FRIGHT OR FLIGHT

Ruskin Bond is known for his signature simplistic and witty writing style. He is the author of several bestselling short stories, novellas, collections, essays and children's books; and has contributed a number of poems and articles to various magazines and anthologies. At the age of twenty-three, he won the prestigious John Llewellyn Rhys Prize for his first novel, *The Room on the Roof*. He was also the recipient of the Padma Shri in 1999, Lifetime Achievement Award by the Delhi Government in 2012, and the Padma Bhushan in 2014.

Born in 1934, Ruskin Bond grew up in Jamnagar, Shimla, New Delhi and Dehradun. Apart from three years in the UK, he has spent all his life in India, and now lives in Landour, Mussoorie, with his adopted family.

FRIGHT OR FLIGHT

Edited & Compiled by
RUSKIN BOND

RUPA

Published by
Rupa Publications India Pvt. Ltd 2018
7/16, Ansari Road, Daryaganj
New Delhi 110002

Sales centres:
Allahabad Bengaluru Chennai
Hyderabad Jaipur Kathmandu
Kolkata Mumbai

Copyright © Ruskin Bond 2018

This is a work of fiction. Names, characters, places and incidents are either the product of the author's imagination or are used fictitiously and any resemblance to any actual person, living or dead, events or locales is entirely coincidental.

All rights reserved.
No part of this publication may be reproduced, transmitted, or stored in a retrieval system, in any form or by any means, electronic, mechanical, photocopying, recording or otherwise, without the prior permission of the publisher.

ISBN: 978-93-5304-069-7

First impression 2018

10 9 8 7 6 5 4 3 2 1

Printed at HT Media Ltd, Gr. Noida

This book is sold subject to the condition that it shall not, by way of trade or otherwise, be lent, resold, hired out, or otherwise circulated, without the publisher's prior consent, in any form of binding or cover other than that in which it is published.

CONTENTS

Introduction	vii
A Fright in the Night *Ruskin Bond*	1
An Underground Episode *Edmund Ware*	5
The Last Match *Edward Fitz-Gerald Flipp*	16
The Haunts of Isabeline *C.H. Donald*	44
Hunting with a Camera *F.W. Champion*	64
The Beast with Five Fingers *W.F. Harvey*	73
First Day in the Life of a Lion Trainer *Patricia Bourne*	106
Escape from Java *Ruskin Bond*	116
Hunters of Souls *Augustus Somerville*	136

Pendlebury's Trophy *John Eyton*	148
The Eye of the Eagle *Ruskin Bond*	160
Mustela of the Lone Hand *C.G.D. Roberts*	170
Beckwith's Case *Maurice Hewlett*	183
When Al Capone was Ambushed *Jack Bilbo*	205

INTRODUCTION

Have you ever woken up in the middle of the night feeling that someone is watching you?

Have you ever broken into a sweat while asleep due to some nightmare?

Have rattling windows ever woken you up at night, even though you remember fastening them tightly before you went to bed?

Are ghosts real? I for one haven't been able to find the answer. But what I have realized over the years is that fear is real. I have myself have felt scared to the bones on several occasions, sometimes even just because of an ivy branch tapping at my window at night.

But phantom stories aren't all that are terrifying. Explorers, hunters, officers lost in the wilderness, soldiers in extreme danger—they have many characteristics in common, including a certain amount of foolhardiness and luck in the stories they have put down. Searching for wild animals in the depths of jungles or coming across terrible rituals in out-of-the-way places, some of these writers have narrated their stories that remain bloodcurdling reads even today.

The stories within the pages of this book are the perfect mix of the terrifying and the adventurous. I have selected these because together they have the ability to seduce the reader and then carrying him or her along by means of a riveting tale which builds up to an exciting climax.

'The Last Match' is a story by a relatively lesser known writer, who tells a simple story built around a difficult, almost impossible situation. The background is authentic, the character real. It's the epic struggle of a woman against the elements. Will she survive the unequal struggle? The reader identifies with the protagonist, and almost wills her into making one last effort in the struggle against Nature's fury.

'Hunters of Souls' too carries an imminent sense of doom and danger as the British visitor to the forests around Daltonganj loses his Indian companions while he faces off with dangerous animals. His companions are not dead though, for he stumbles upon a ritual carried out by soul hunters where the companions play a crucial role. As he watches on in horror, wondering when he may step in to the rescue, he witnesses a hidden ceremony and a messy secret of those who remained outside the control of the British Raj.

'Hunting with a Camera' is from the period when the walls of almost every official or civil residence were adorned with the mounted heads of tiger and panther, or the antlers of chital, sambhur or antelope. Everyone who entered the jungle went in with guns blazing. F.W. Champion of the Indian Forest Service was a pioneering wildlife photographer who preferred to do his shooting with a camera. His works reveal knowledge of the jungle, wildlife and natural history equal to that of Jim Corbett and Kenneth Anderson.

Also included here are three of my own stories—'A Fright in the Night', 'Escape from Java' and 'The Eye of the Eagle'—rubbing shoulders with writers like C.H. Donald, W.F. Harvey,

Augustus Somerville, John Eyton, and many others.

I have always believed that there are two kinds of people—those who get a thrill by standing in the face of danger and physically experiencing adventures; and those who get equally thrilled or scared by reading tales of horror and adventure while snuggled warmly in bed with a cup of tea. I belong to the latter category. And you?

Ruskin Bond

A FRIGHT IN THE NIGHT

Ruskin Bond

Our elderly school nurse, Miss Babcock, passed away quite suddenly one autumn evening, apparently of a heart attack. She was laid out on her camp bed in the little room adjoining our four-bed hospital ward. The funeral would be held next day.

Tata and I were school prefects that year, and we both knew Miss Babcock quite well, having often feigned stomach aches or sore throats in order to escape morning PT (physical training) or extra maths periods. It wasn't really a hospital, just a sick bay for the usual cases of measles or mumps. Anyone who went down with something really serious would be sent to Simla's Ripon Hospital.

Mr Fisher, our headmaster, summoned Tata and me to his office.

'Bond,' he said. 'You liked Miss Babcock, didn't you?'

'Yes, sir.'

'And you, Tata?'

'She was a good sport, sir.'

'Good. And since you are both familiar with the hospital, having got yourselves admitted whenever possible, I think it only right that you should be given the duty of keeping a vigil for

2 Fright or Flight

Miss Babcock. It's not good to leave the dead alone all night. All you have to do is spend the night beside her bed. Keep the rats away! You can take turns. From nine to midnight, Bond will be on duty. After that, Tata will take over. There's a spare bed in the ward, and an easy chair in the bedroom. Now have your supper, and then go down to the hospital and relieve Mr Jones, who has been there all evening.'

Mr Jones was happy to be able to return to arranging his stamp collection, and wished us a comfortable night in the company of Miss Babcock.

The old lady looked peaceful enough stretched out on her camp bed. She was covered in a bedsheet and only her face and hands were visible. Someone had tried to close her eyes but they remained only half shut.

'Don't try anything funny,' said Tata. 'I think she's watching us.'

'She's been dead for hours,' I said. 'You go and lie down. I'll wake you up at twelve.'

Tata returned to the ward, and I sat down in the easy chair near Miss Babcock's bed. It was a still, silent night, the only sound being the ticking of a wall clock in a corner of the room. A small light bulb glowed over the dressing table. But in those days we were subject to power failures just as we are today, and presently the bulb went out and we were plunged into darkness.

But not for long.

Presently, a full moon came up over the mountains, flooding the garden with moonlight. A moonbeam crept in at the window and moved slowly across the room. Outside, a nightjar honked.

I had been watching Miss Babcock's peaceful countenance for some time, wondering if her spirit was hovering around the room, keeping a watch over me even as I kept a watch over her. In the dark I could only make out the outline of her face, but as the moonlight crept across her bed, I began to make out her features.

Presently the moonlight rested on her face. I could see all her features quite distinctly.

And then, to my horror, she began to smile at me.

A corpse smiling at you in the middle of the night is not the most pleasant of experiences. It is calculated to give you goosebumps. And when the smile becomes an evil grimace, it is time to say your prayers.

But there was no time for prayer. The smile widened even further, and then, with a loud bang—somewhat like a firecracker going off—Miss Babcock's set of false teeth shot out of her mouth and landed on the bedsheet.

At the same time I shot out of my chair and fled from the room, calling to Tata for help.

'She's alive!' I cried. 'Miss Babcock's after me!'

Tata leapt out of bed, peeked into Miss Babcock's room, saw her grinning face, and came back shouting, 'Let's get Fishy!' ('Fishy' being short for our headmaster, Mr Fisher.) 'Before she starts screaming at us!'

Together we rushed up the hospital steps and down the path to the headmaster's house. The headmaster dragged Mr Jones away from his stamp collection, and the four of us tramped down to the hospital, fully expecting to find Miss Babcock walking about.

But she was still laid out, and still very much dead—according to Mr Jones, who'd been in the army and seen many dead people.

'We forgot to take her teeth out,' he explained, indicating

Miss Babcock's false teeth which had popped out during my vigil. 'When rigor mortis set in, and her jaw stiffened, the teeth were forced out.'

'They came out with a lot of noise, sir,' I said, still shaken up. 'And she was grinning at me all the time.'

'Well, we know you're a funny fellow, Bond,' said Mr Fisher, giving me one of his own sarcastic smiles. 'Even a corpse can't help grinning at you!'

Tata and I were excused from further 'invigilation', and sent back to our dormitories, where we regaled everyone with a hair-raising account of our experience.

This is a perfectly true story; but it is not really a ghost story.

I think I would prefer seeing a ghost to sitting up with a corpse late into the night.

AN UNDERGROUND EPISODE

Edmund Ware

Three figures leaned against the slanting rain—Alamo Laska, Nick Christopher, and the boy who had run away from home. They rested on their long-handled shovels and, as they gazed into the crater which by their brawn they had hollowed in the earth, the blue clay oozed back again, slowly devouring the fruits of their toil.

Laska, the nomad, thought of the wild geese winging southward to warm bayous. Nick's heart, under the bone and muscle of his great chest, swelled with sweet thoughts of his wife and child who lived in a foreign city across an ocean. The boy felt the sting of rain against his cheeks and dreamed of his mother who seemed lovely and far away.

It was Sunday. The regular deep-trench gang lounged in their warm boarding house and drank dago red, while out on the job the three men toiled alone. They breathed heavily, and the gray steam crawled upon their backs, for it was cold.

'Look at 'er filling in,' growled Laska, 'faster than a man could dig.'

'Mud's get inna pipe,' said Nick. 'The Inspector make us tear him out if she fill any more.'

Backed close to the edge of the crater stood a giant trench-digging machine. In the dusk it appeared as a crouched and shadowy animal—silent, gloomy, capable. But a broken piston had crippled its engines and they were swathed in tarpaulin.

A long gray mound stretched away from the crater opposite the machine. Buried thirty feet below the mound was the new-laid sewer pipe. From the bottom of the pit at the machine, the pipe ran a hundred yards horizontally under the surface, opening in a manhole. This hundred yards of new-laid pipe was the reason for the three men digging in the rain. They had dug eleven hours trying to uncover the open end of the pipe in order to seal it against the mud. But rain and ooze and storm had bested them. The bank had caved, and the mud had crawled into the mouth of the pipe, obstructing it.

'It's getting dark fast,' said Laska, 'an' we're licked.'

'We can't do nothing more,' said the boy.

Nick Christopher scraped the mud from his shovel. He looked up into the Whirlpools of the sky. 'In a year I go old country. I see my wife. I see my kid.'

'Nick,' said Laska, 'go over to the 'shanty and get a couple of lanterns and telephone Stender. Tell him if he don't want the Inspector on our tail to get out here quick with a gang.'

Nick stuck his shovel in the mud and moved away across the plain toward the shanty.

The cold had crept into the boy. It frightened him, and in the darkness his eyes sought Laska's face. 'How could we clean out the pipe, even when the gang got down to it?'

'Maybe we could flush her out with a fire hose,' said Laska.

'There's no water plug within a mile.'

Laska said nothing. The boy waited for him to reply, but he didn't. Picking up his damp shirt, the boy pulled it on over his head. He did not tuck in the tails, and they flapped in the wind, slapping against him. He looked like a gaunt, serious bird, striving to leave the ground. He was bare-headed, and his yellow hair was matted and stringy with dampness. His face was thin, a little sunken, and fine drops of moisture clung to the fuzz on his cheeks. His lips were blue with cold. He was seventeen.

Laska stared into the pit. It was too dark to see the bottom, but something in the black hole fascinated him. 'If we could get a rope through the pipe we could drag sandbags through into the manhole. That would clean her out in good shape.'

'How could we get a rope through?'

'I dunno. Stender'll know.' Laska walked over to the digging machine and leaned against its towering side. The rain had turned to sleet. 'It's cold,' he said.

The boy followed Laska, and went close to him for warmth and friendship. 'How *could* we get a rope through?'

Laska's shoulders lifted slowly. 'You'll see. You'll see when Stender gets here. Say, it's freezing.'

After a long time of waiting, a yellow light flamed into being in the shanty, and they heard the muffled scraping of boots on the board floor. The shanty door opened. A rectangle of light stood out sharply.

Swart figures crossed and recrossed the lighted area, pouring out into the storm.

'Ho!' called Laska.

'Ho!' came the answer, galloping to them in the wind.

They heard the rasping of caked mud on dungarees, the clank of shovels, the voice of Stender, the foreman. Lanterns swung like yellow pendulums. Long-legged shadows reached and receded.

The diggers gathered about the rim of the pit, staring. Stender's face showed in the lantern light. His lips were wrinkled, as if constantly prepared for blasphemy. He was a tall, cursing conqueror. Orders shot from his throat, and noisily the men descended into the pit and began to dig. They drew huge, gasping breaths like mired beasts fighting for life.

The boy watched, his eyes bulging in the dark. Hitherto he had thought very briefly of sewers, regarding them as unlovely things. But Laska and Nick and Stender gave them splendour and importance. The deep-trench men were admirable monsters. They knew the clay, the feel and pattern of it, for it had long been heavy in their minds and muscles. They were big in three dimensions and their eyes were black and barbarous. When they ate it was with rough-and-tumble relish, and as their bellies fattened, they spoke tolerantly of enemies. They played lustily with a view to satiation. They worked stupendously. They were diggers in clay, transformed by lantern light into a race of giants.

Through the rain came Stender, his black slicker crackling. 'They're down,' he said. 'Angelo just struck the pipe.'

Laska grunted.

Stender blew his nose with his fingers, walked away, and climbed down into the hole. They lost sight of him as he dropped over the rim. The sound of digging had ceased and two or three men on the surface rested on their shovels, the light from below gleaming in their flat faces. Laska and the boy knew that Stender was examining the pipe. They heard him swearing at what he had found.

After a moment he clambered up over the rim and held up a lantern. His cuddy, gripped firmly between his teeth, was upside down to keep out the wet.

'Someone's got to go through the pipe,' he said, raising his voice. 'There's fifty bucks for the man that'll go through the pipe into the manhole with a line tied to his foot. Fifty bucks!'

There was a moment of quiet. The men thought of the fifty dollars and furtively measured themselves against the deed at hand. It seemed to the boy that he was the only one who feared the task. He did not think of the fifty dollars, but thought only of the fear. Three hundred feet through a rathole, eighteen inches in diameter. Three hundred feet of muck, of wet black dark, and no turning back. But, if he did not volunteer, they would know that he was afraid. The boy stepped from behind Laska and said uncertainly: 'I'll go, Stender,' and he wished he might snatch back the words; for, looking about him, he saw that not a man among those present could have wedged his shoulders into the mouth of an eighteen-inch pipe. He was the only volunteer. They had known he would be the only one.

Stender came striding over holding the lantern above his head. He peered into the boy's face. 'Take off your clothes,' he said.

'Take off my clothes?'

'That's what I said.'

'You might get a buckle caught in a joint,' said Laska. 'See?'

The boy saw only that he had been trapped very cunningly. At home he could have been openly fearful, for at home everything about him was known. There, quite simply, he could have said: 'I won't do it. I'm frightened. I'll be killed.' But here the diggers in clay were lancing him with looks. And Laska was bringing a ball of line, one end of which would be fastened to his ankle.

'Just go in a sweater,' said Laska. 'A sweater an' boots over your woolens. We'll be waiting for you at the manhole.'

He wanted so desperately to dive off into the night that he felt his legs bracing for a spring, and a tight feeling in his throat. Then, mechanically, he began to take off his clothes. Nick had gone clumping off to the shanty and shortly he returned with a pair of hip boots. 'Here, kid. I get 'em warm for you inna shanty.'

He thrust his feet into the boots, and Laska knelt and tied the heavy line to his ankle. 'Too tight?'

'No. It's all right, I guess.'

'Well—come on.

They walked past Stender who was pacing up and down among the men. They slid down into the crater, deepened now by the diggers. They stood by the partly covered mouth of the pipe. They were thirty feet below the surface of the ground.

Laska reached down and tugged at the knot he had tied in the line, then he peered into the mouth of the tube. He peered cautiously, as if he thought it might be inhabited. The boy's glance wandered up the wet sides of the pit. Over the rim a circle of bland yellow faces peered at him. Sleet tinkled against lanterns, spattered down and stung his flesh.

'Go ahead in,' said Laska.

The boy blanched.

'Just keep thinking of the manhole, where you'll come out,' said Laska.

The boy's throat constricted. He seemed to be bursting with a pressure from inside. He got down on his belly in the slush-ice and mud. It penetrated slowly to his skin and spread over him. He put his head inside the mouth of the pipe, drew back in horror. Some gibbering words flew from his lips. His voice sounded preposterously loud. Laska's voice was already shopworn with distance. 'You can make it! Go ahead.'

He lay on his left side, and, reaching out with his left arm, caught a joint and drew himself in. The mud oozed up around him, finding its way upon him, welling up against the left side of his face. He pressed his right cheek against the ceiling of the pipe to keep the muck from covering his mouth and nose. Laska's voice was far and muffled. Laska was in another world—a sane world of night, of storm, and the mellow glow of lanterns.

'Are you makin' it all right, kid?'

The boy cried out, his ears ringing with his cry. It re-echoed from the sides of the pipe. The sides hemmed him, pinned him, close him in on every side with their paralysing circumference.

There is no darkness like the darkness underground that miners know. It borrows something from night, from tombs, from places used by bats. Such fluid black can terrify a flame, and suffocate and drench a mind with madness. There is a fierce desire to struggle, to beat one's hands against the prison.

The boy longed to lift his pitiful human strength against the walls. He longed to claw at his eyes in the mad certainty that more than darkness curtained them.

He had moved but a few feet on his journey when panic swept him. Ahead of him the mud had built into a stolid wave. Putting forth his left hand, he felt a scant two inches between the wave's crest and the ceiling of the pipe. There was nothing to do but go back. If he moved ahead, it meant death by suffocation. He tried to back away, but caught his toe in a joint of the pipe. He was entombed! In an hour he would be a body. The cold and dampness would kill him before they could dig down to him. Nick and Laska would pull him from the muck, and Laska would say: 'Huh, his clock's stopped.'

He thrashed with delirious strength against his prison. He felt the skin tearing from the backs of his hands as he flailed the rough walls. And some gods must have snickered, for above the walls of the pipe were thirty feet of unyielding clay, eight thousand miles of earth below. A strength, a weight, a night, each a thousand times his most revolting dream, leaned upon the boy, depressing, crushing, stamping him out. The ground gave no cry of battle. It did no bleeding, suffered no pain, uttered no groans. It flattened him silently. It swallowed him in its foul despotism. It dropped its merciless weight upon his mind. It was so inhuman, so horribly incognizant of the God men swore had made it.

In the midst of his frenzy, when he had beaten his face against the walls until it bled, he heard a ringing voice he knew was real, springing from human sympathy. It was Laska, calling: 'Are you all right, kid?'

In that instant the boy loved Laska as he loved his life. Laska's voice sheered the weight from him, scattered the darkness, brought him new balance and a hope to live.

'Fine!' he answered in a cracking yell. He yelled again, loving the sound of his voice, and thinking how foolish yelling was in such a place.

With his left hand he groped ahead and found that the wave of mud had settled, levelled off by its own weight. He drew his body together, pressing it against the pipe. He straightened, moved ahead six inches. His fingers found a loop of oakum dangling from a joint, and he pulled himself on, his left arm forward, his right arm behind over his hip, like a swimmer's.

He had vanquished panic, and he looked ahead to victory. Each joint brought him twenty inches nearer his goal. Each twenty inches was a plateau which enabled him to vision a new plateau—the next joint. The joints were like small deceitful rests upon a march.

He had been more than an hour on the way. He did not know how far he had gone, a third, perhaps even a half of the distance. He forgot the present, forgot fear, wet, cold, blackness; he lost himself in dreaming of the world of men outside the prison. It was as if he were a small superb island in hell.

He did not know how long he had been counting the joints, but he found himself whispering good numbers: 'Fifty-one, fifty-two, fifty-three...' Each joint, when he thought of it, appeared to take up a vast time of squirming in the muck, and the line dragged heavily behind his foot.

Suddenly, staring into the darkness so that it seemed to bring a pain to his eyes, he saw a pallid ray. He closed his eyes, opened them, and looked again. The ray was real, and he uttered a whimper of relief. He knew that the ray must come from Stender's lantern. He pictured Stender and a group of the diggers huddled in the manhole, waiting for him. The men and the manhole grew magnificent in his mind, and he thought of them worshipfully.

'Seventy-six, seventy-seven, seventy-eight....'

The ray grew slowly, like a worthwhile thing. It took an oval shape, and the oval grew fat, like an eg, then round. It was a straight line to the manhole, and the mud had thinned.

Through the pipe, into the boy's ears, a voice rumbled like half-hearted thunder. It was Stender's voice: 'How you makin' it?'

'Oh, just fine!' His cry came pricking back into his ears like a shower of needles.

There followed a long span of numbness. The cold and wet had dulled his senses, so that whenever the rough ceiling of the pipe ripped his face, he did not feel it; so that struggling in the muck became an almost pleasant and normal thing, since all elements of fear and pain and imagination had been removed. Warmth and dryness became alien to him. He was a creature native to darkness, foreign to light.

The round yellow disc before him gave him his only sense of living. It was a sunlit landfall, luring him on. He would close his eyes and count five joints, then open them quickly, cheering himself at the perceptible stages of progress.

Then, abruptly, it seemed, he was close to the manhole. He could hear men moving. He could see the outline of Stender's head as Stender peered into the mouth of the pipe. Men kneeled, pushing each other's heads to one side, in order to watch him squirm toward them. They began to talk excitedly. He could hear them breathing, see details—and Stender and Laska reached in. They got their hands upon him. They hauled him to them, as if he were something they wanted to inspect scientifically. He felt as if they thought he was a rarity, a thing of great oddness. The light dazzled him. It began to move around and around, and to dissolve into many lights, some of which danced locally on a bottle. He heard Stender's voice: 'Well, he made it all right. What do you know?'

'Here, kid,' said Laska, holding the bottle to his mouth. 'Drink all of this that you can hold.'

He could not stand up. He believed calmly that his flesh and bones were constructed of putty. He could hear no vestige of the song of victory he had dreamed of hearing. He looked stupidly at his hands, which bled painlessly. He could not feel his arms and legs at all. He was a vast sensation of lantern light and the steam of human beings breathing in a damp place.

Faces peered at him. The faces were curious and surprised. He felt a clouded, uncomprehending resentment against them. Stender held him up on one side, Laska on the other. They looked at each other across him. Suddenly Laska stooped and gathered him effortlessly into his arms.

'You'll get covered with mud,' mumbled the boy.

'Damn if he didn't make it all right,' said Stender. 'Save us tearing out the pipe.'

'Hell with the pipe,' said Laska.

The boy's wet head fell against Laska's chest. He felt the rise and fall of Laska's muscles, and knew that Laska was climbing with him up the iron steps inside the manhole. Night wind smote him. He buried his head deeper against Laska. Laska's body became a mountain of warmth. He felt a heavy sighing peace, like a soldier who has been comfortably wounded and knows that war for him is over.

THE LAST MATCH

Edward Fitz-Gerald Flipp

'Well, I guess we'd better be hitting for home. I don't like the smell of that wind. She's going to blizz before long, or I miss my guess.'

'By golly, I believe you're right. A dollar, fifty. That's right. Goodbye, Mr Mawson. Goodbye, Mrs Mills.'

The owner of the feed company dumped the sack of corn meal behind the seat, Mawson clicked his tongue to his horse and the cutter moved off up the one street of Sunset with a merry jingling of sleigh bells.

The little prairie town was half-asleep under its mantle of snow, for it was the third winter since the slump in wheat. For three years the price of No. 1 Northern had hovered round sixty cents on the Winnipeg Grain Exchange, and times were hard: harder than anyone could remember, butter being used for axle grease and eggs fed direct to the pigs for lack of a better market.

The neighbouring farmers no longer thronged into Sunset on Saturdays in their cars. One of the two garages was closed, and the other only employed one man instead of four. The cinema gave one performance a week, and the Rex Café and the Good Eats Café had an occasional customer. The stores were listless, and Ed Wilson's barber's shop and pool-room were nearly empty. This latter fact proved the severity of the depression beyond any doubt, for when the pool-room is empty, times are hard indeed. Not even the farmers themselves scanned the news of the Winnipeg Grain Exchange with greater eagerness than did the storekeepers and merchants of Sunset. Wheat was no longer king when No. 1 Northern was only sixty cents a bushel.

Within a minute or two the cutter had left the little town behind, and the main street of Sunset had given place to a long straight road, stretching endlessly and always perfectly straight across the bald prairie. Behind them the grain elevator reared its white height into the air, watching over Sunset as the church spire watches over the villages of older lands.

For some time the man and woman drove in silence, wrapped in the warm buffalo robe which keeps out any draughts. The noise of the horse's hoofs was deadened by the snow, and the only sound was the jingling of the sleigh bells. Talk held no attraction for either of them; talk meant discussion of the price of wheat, and No. 1 Northern was only sixty cents in Winnipeg.

At last Mawson spoke:

'Seems queer to be driving in a cutter again. Takes me back to before the war. I guess we'd all have been better off if we'd never had any cars; but once you've had one, you kind a seem lost without it. A rig seems so slow.'

'It certainly does,' she answered, and they drove on in silence.

The winter had been extraordinarily mild without one sub-zero spell. For the last two days it had been snowing with a slight south wind: a steady fall of what the prairie calls wet snow (though, even so, far drier than any which ever falls in England). The air was still full of white flakes, falling silently and yet at the same time making a gentle, almost imperceptible, patter as they settled on their hats and on the buffalo robe, which was now altogether white where it covered their knees.

The trail they had made driving into Sunset was vague and nearly obliterated. It was hard work for the horse breaking a fresh track, and progress was slow. The flakes of snow seemed to be growing smaller and falling faster, and, though they had blown into their faces during the drive into Sunset, now on the return trip they still blew slantwise against them.

'I don't like the smell of it,' Mawson muttered. 'The wind's backed to the north and that sure means something.' He raised his voice and called, 'Git on there, Pete.'

Pete shook his ears and settled his shoulders into the traces. He needed no urging, for he, too, had felt the change of wind and wanted to get back to his stable.

Gradually the gusts increased in force. On the drive in it had been pleasant to feel the south wind driving the soft flakes against their faces. They had felt almost warm as they touched the cheek.

But there was a bite in this new wind. There was no doubt now that the flakes had grown much smaller. They grew smaller every minute until they were tiny atoms blowing straight against them in a line almost parallel with the ground. The wind, coming in a sweep across hundreds of miles of barren tundra in the Arctic Circle, without a single obstacle in the way to lessen its force, brought a wave of cold that made them shiver.

Already the mercury in thermometers on the international boundary was beginning to fall. By midnight it would be falling in the cities of the middle United States, and by midnight twenty-four hours later workers on cotton plantations in the Mississippi Valley, 2,000 miles to the south, would be shivering as the tail end of the storm reached them, tamed at last after its swoop across the prairies.

Presently the tiny flakes of snow began to sting their faces. As the gusts increased the snow came in swirling clouds, rather as though someone was shaking the folds of a gigantic white carpet. During these gusts it was impossible to see more than a few yards ahead, and the sense of direction was lost as in a fog. Almost it seemed that the snow was a fog, so dry it was, filtering like a fog into tiny gaps in the clothing. It crept between the top of the gloves and the sleeve of the overcoat and down the gap between muffler and coat collar.

The wind, devoid of moisture, dried the snow which had already fallen, whirling it up into twisting spirals to join the horizontal sweep of the driven flakes. It drove the light powder against the slightest obstacles, so that each fence post was covered for a few inches on its windward side. By morning they would be nearly buried in the drifts, whose nucleus they were forming.

The man and woman sat closer together on the seat of the cutter, their heads thrust forward so that the snow would have less chance of seeping down their necks. He raised his hands to pull down his ear-flaps, and the snow fell off his mittens like powdered salt. Not a single flake had stuck to them, it was so dry.

At length Mawson indulged in the gloomy satisfaction of a prophet whose words have come true.

'I knew I could smell a blizzard coming,' he said. 'It's lucky we weren't two hours later. I guess your husband ought to be safely in the shack by now.'

She turned to answer him, and the movement allowed the wind to blow all the snow from her hat.

'Yes, he'll be all right. Reckoned he'd reach there by three.'

She bent her head to face the wind again, and they drove in silence. Her husband had left home at four o'clock that morning to drive to the bush, which began in sheltered bluffs to the north of them. The northern prairie gives way to belts of semi-stunted trees where the ground holds more moisture.

With No. 1 Northern only sixty cents a bushel in Winnipeg the farmer cannot afford to buy coal, and her husband and a neighbour had gone to cut a year's supply of fuel in the poplar bluffs. Later they would have to haul it thirty miles to their homes, sitting on top of their loads as the sleighs crossed the snowy plain, the thermometer below zero and as likely as not a bitter wind numbing them in body and mind.

The cutter was approaching a house standing a little back from the road; a gaunt, unpainted, wooden house without any pretensions to adornment. It was simply an enclosed rectangle, with a front door and a back door and four rooms, and the necessary windows to admit light: a house rather than a home, a place in which to eat and sleep and take shelter from the weather, like most of the other houses on prairie farms.

It rose straight from the flat field. There was no hedge, no railings, no lawn, no flower garden, to separate it from the wheat-land. Close beside it was a huge barn, dwarfing the house as the farm dwarfed the human beings who worked it.

Mawson drove up to the back door, and the woman got out, taking with her a shallow, open, wooden box which had once contained cans of condensed milk. It was now piled with brown-paper parcels, the groceries for which she had traded her butter, and underneath was her mail. The parcels were covered with a thick powder of snow which had filtered in under the buffalo robe, filling up the spaces between them till they looked like one amorphous lump.

'Thanks for driving me in,' she shouted.

'Aw, shucks, that's nothing. You're sure you'll be all right alone?'

'Yes, Jim fixed up everything before he left.'

'Have you got everything?' he asked.

'Yes,' she shouted as a gust, fiercer than any which had come before, enveloped them in swirling white.

It blew the tiny flakes into their eyes and ears and down their necks, and lifted a cloud from the box that for a minute blinded them. She had a fleeting impression that one of the top parcels had blown into the drift already forming; but when she was able to see again and looked at the box, it was once more covered white. And the snow round them looked just as it had done.

She was half-frozen and wanted to gain the warmth of the house; Pete was pawing his feet, longing to be on the way to his stable, and she knew it was not wise for Mawson to linger, He had three more miles to go before he reached home, and if he did not go quickly he might be badly frostbitten, as the blizzard was increasing every minute.

She looked at her box again. It seemed just the same. She must have been mistaken in thinking that anything had been blown out of it. Even if it had, it would make no difference. She would never find it until the spring, and in any case there was plenty of food in the house.

Mawson, plainly anxious to be off, again asked: 'You're sure you're all right?'

'Yes,' she shouted, 'and thanks a lot for the lift.'

He waved his hand, and Pete seized the opportunity to dash forward. In a moment the cutter was lost to view in the driving snow, and she turned hurriedly to the door.

From the uncovered rafters of the veranda hung quantities of meat impaled on hooks, cuts of veal and pork, for her husband had lately killed a calf and a pig.

That is one good thing about the prairie winter, she thought, as she ran up the three steps. You killed a pig, simply hung up the meat and then it froze immediately, and stayed frozen until you wanted it. Pretty convenient, and they were lucky to have so much in hard times.

The snow had drifted against the back door, half-hiding the washing-machine and brooms leaning against the wall. All the rest of the veranda floor was bare, every particle of dirt dried into dust and swept away by the wind; the boards looked as if they had been scrubbed.

She had no need to search for a key. You do not lock your door on the prairie when you go away for the day. She kicked the drift with a sweep of her foot, and it disappeared in a fine mist, which swirled up into her face and vanished as the wind sucked it away.

She pulled the door open quickly, and almost jumped into the kitchen in her haste to enter before another drift could accumulate and blow in after her.

What a relief to be out of that biting wind! The kitchen was almost eerie with its comparative warmth and silence after the buffeting outside. It felt curious to be there alone without her husband, even frightening with the blizzard increasing in fury. For a moment the prospect appalled her, but she was the wife of a prairie farmer and resolutely thrust off her depression.

A gust of wind, which seemed as if it would carry away the whole house, sent an icy blast under the door and through the keyhole. It was a warning not to waste time. She had to milk yet, and it would not be safe to cross the corral in the dark. A second, gust roused her to action.

Lifting the lid of the stove, she saw there was a little pile of embers. She snatched two sticks of wood from the box and thrust them into the opening, pulling back the draught as she did so. The two bedrooms and the sitting-room were warmed by a box heater, but owing to the warm weather of the two previous days she had not lighted it in her efforts to economize.

She looked hesitatingly at it, for it would be so comforting to come back to a thoroughly warm house after the frozen barn, but another roar of wind made her resist the temptation, The intensity of the storm was terrifying, and she knew both from experience and from warning that she must be back in the house before it was dark, the heater would have to wait.

She took off her good coat and hat, shook the snow off them and flung them on a chair. The loneliness of the empty room began to affect her nerves. It was more lonely than she had thought it would be, and the noises of the blizzard intensified the loneliness until she felt flustered and a little panic-stricken at the thought of the solitary vigil before her.

Her one idea now was haste—haste to get done with the milking and then to come back to the task of keeping the house warm, and its precious supply of vegetables in the cellar.

She put on her woollen blizzard-cap so that it reached halfway down her neck and left only a tiny opening for eyes and nose. Next she put on an old farm overcoat, fastening the collar over the lower part of her blizzard-cap so that there was no chance of her neck being frozen. Then her woollen mittens, and over them the buckskin outer mittens.

No fear of frostbite now for a little while; but she had to hurry. Every second was of importance. Should she leave the draught on in the stove to make sure of the wood catching? If she did, it would probably all have burnt away by the time she came back. She could not wait to give it more time. It would soon be dark. The wood was dry and must have caught by this time, and it always burnt easily in zero weather.

Without pausing to look in her flurry, she thrust back the damper with her thumb. It closed with a clang and she hurried to the door, taking a kettle with her.

It was all she could do to open the door. The wind and cold made her gasp for breath, and a cloud of snow like the finest powder blew past her into the room. The door slammed behind her, and she picked up her milk-pail from beside the washing-machine.

For a moment she almost quailed. It was still light, but she could hardly see the huge barn although it was only fifty yards away. The air seemed to be a mass of tiny, white missiles flying towards her at the speed of an express train. They stung like needles on her eyes and nose, and she could feel them whipping past her legs. Mercifully she had put on her felt boots before going to Sunset. Her feet would have been frozen in leather ones.

She must hurry! If she let it get dark before she finished milking she would never find the house on the way back.

The well was in a straight line between the house and the barn door, otherwise she would not have found it. She stumbled forward with her shoulders thrust in front and her head bent downward to protect her eyes from the stinging snow. Her breath came in painful gasps.

Her milk bucket knocked against the pump handle before she saw the well. She lifted the handle, and, pouring the warm water from her kettle down the pipe, pumped vigorously. Even above the wind she could hear the noise of the suction as her warm water primed the pump and drew the water upwards from the well.

She filled her milk bucket and the other bucket beside the pump. Then she lifted the handle again, and the trip action allowed the water to sink to the bottom of the well so that the pump could not freeze and burst. Her cows could only have one bucket each that night, for there was no time to go back to the house for another kettle.

With her kettle and the two buckets she staggered to the barn, buffeted by the storm and desperately afraid of spilling the water. She was gasping by the time she reached shelter. It was ecstasy to draw breath out of that wind.

There was a drift nearly three feet deep by the barn, where the snow had blown back in an eddy and come to rest in the calm. She ploughed her way through it, holding her buckets high, and the snow fell away from her boots. It was almost like going into an oven after the cold of the wind. The cows looked round from their stalls and lowed at her.

She set one bucket before the first cow, and, in spite of her urge for haste, held it while the animal drank. It would be sure to knock it over if left. Already during the time she had walked twenty-five yards a film of ice had formed on the top of the water.

The cow sniffed and snorted and blew through its nose with exasperating deliberation before it would drink. She wanted to scream to make it hurry, but she forced herself to wait patiently. At last it thrust out an exploring tongue, and after splashing the water for a minute sucked the bucket dry without lifting its head.

When she took the bucket away the cow lowed for more. She spoke soothingly to it and watered the other cow. It drank with equally maddening deliberation, and then she ran to the pile of oat hay her husband had set in readiness for her. She placed several sheaves in the mangers, so that they should not go hungry in case she were late in the morning.

Next she took the heavy scoop shovel and prepared to clean out the gutters; but when she pushed it against the manure the handle jarred against her hands as though she had struck a granite rock. During the short time the storm had been raging the manure had frozen solid. It would take a pick-axe to move it now.

She gave up the attempt, and placed forkfuls of bedding round the cows' legs. They would need it all before the night was through. Already tiny icicles had formed on their nostrils. She could feel the wool of her blizzard-cap as solid as a board where her own breath had caught when she gasped in the wind. It rubbed against her lip irritatingly, and made her all the more conscious of the need to hurry. She snatched the milking-stool, and, tearing off her mittens, put them in her pocket, picked up the milk bucket and hurried to the first cow, but suddenly cried out with pain.

The metal of the handle had torn all the skin from the fingers of her left hand where they had grasped it. She cried with pain and vexation at her mistake. Fool that she was! As if she did not know enough to remember that any metal would tear off the skin in zero weather!

She carried the bucket on the crook of her arm and sat down beside the cow. It was good to thrust her head into its flank and feel the warmth coming from its body.

She could not wash the udder, as she usually did, or it would be covered with icicles. With her right hand she pulled away the scraps of bedding adhering to it, and then began to milk. The skin was torn from the fingers of her left hand just where she used them to squeeze the teats, and every movement hurt excruciatingly. When she lifted them for a moment to ease them there was a smear of blood on the teat. She felt dizzy at the sight of it, but forced herself to begin again.

Gradually she absorbed some warmth from the cow's body and felt the icy teats grow warmer under her fingers. The milk streamed into the bucket between her knees, and the homely, everyday sound of it was soothing. It encouraged her to tell herself that she would only have to do what she had to do every day when her husband was at home; but all her reasoning could not exorcise the terrors suggested by her subconscious mind. What she had to do was not the same as usual, for the simple reason that she was all alone and no one nearer to her than the Mawsons in the next house three miles away.

The sound of the milk streaming into her bucket was becoming drowned by the noise of the wind, and, though the front of her body and her hands were fairly warm, being close to the cow, her back was freezing where the draught from the door and windows struck her.

She shivered a little, and, having milked the rear teats dry, started on the front ones. With the change of position her skinned fingers hurt worse than ever, and the pain increased the tension of her nerves. It was beginning to grow dusk inside the barn. In spite of her injured fingers she milked furiously; for the idea that she must regain the house before it was dark was all the more terrifying because she knew it was justified and not a mere product of her fears. But the knowledge that it was justified made her still more highly strung.

At last! She had milked the cow dry. She gave a sigh of relief and crooked her arm under the handle of the bucket.

She could not bring herself to milk the other cow. It was

going dry soon in any case. It would not hurt to be missed this once.

She pulled on her mittens, wincing as the wool pressed against her injured fingers, then unfastened the chains from the cows' necks that they might lie down against each other when they had finished eating, and so keep warm.

Now to gain the house and her own cosy kitchen once more. There were the papers to read and the letters from her husband's English relations, whom she would never see unless wheat was worth a great deal more than sixty cents a bushel for No. 1 Northern.

She felt she could not wait another minute. The chickens had a self-feeding hopper and enough to eat till morning. In any case they would be huddled shivering on their perches. She had finished! Now for a roaring fire in the stove and the heater. She would sit close to the stove and eat her supper, and read her letters and the papers, and be so comfortable that she would forget the terror of being alone. Above all, she would be warm. She would be warm even if she had to sit on top of the stove.

With the kettle and the pail of milk she hurried to the door. Cold as it was in the barn, it was far colder outside. The noise of the wind, which had been muffled inside the building, made her gasp with fear at its fury. It was not so dark, though, as she had expected, and she gave a sigh of thankfulness for this, because the house was practically invisible through the whirling maelstrom of snow. All the usual landmarks were changed, and if she had been twenty minutes later she would never have found her way.

The first two feet of ground by the barn door were still bare, but the drift had formed again where the snow blew back in the eddy. It had re-formed into a bank exactly like a wave with the crest as sharp as a knife. There was not the slightest sign of her footmarks where she had walked twenty minutes earlier.

She ploughed her way homeward, the wind at her back. It almost lifted her off her feet, the bucket of milk tugged forward at her arm, and she could hear the unceasing rustle of the snow as it rushed past her legs like an incredibly swift river. She knew she could never have walked a hundred yards against it.

It was unspeakable relief to feel her feet once more on the veranda steps. She had regained the house after all, and before her eyes floated a vision of a red-hot stove, with the kettle boiling and the teapot warming and a joint of pork sizzling in the oven. She would eat hot pork and drink boiling tea and heap the butter on her bread, and the fat would keep her warm— warm right through her shoulders and the back of her knees where the wind was cutting.

In the centre of the veranda steps the snow had drifted into a cone a foot high, but on both sides the boards were absolutely bare. Half of the veranda was still bare, but against the wall and the door there was a bank of snow. As she reached the door she glanced at the thermometer hanging on the wall. It showed twenty degrees below zero. From that she knew it would be forty below at six o'clock the next morning. Seventy-two degrees of frost! An idle fancy made her wonder how she could convey an idea of that cold to her husband's relations in England. Seventy-two degrees above freezing meant a hundred and four in the shade, hotter than it ever was in London even on the hottest day of the hottest summer. Could they imagine a temperature the same number of degrees below freezing?

At this fancy she smiled for the first time since Mawson had left her, and swept her foot at the pile of snow by the door. It was sucked up past her face and out beyond the angle of the house as if it had been a cloud of smoke from a bonfire.

With thankfulness she heard the door slam behind her. She was home. In a few minutes the stove would be roaring and red-hot, and then she would be warm. Warm! At the thought of it her tautened nerves relaxed.

She set down her bucket and ran to the stove. It did not feel as warm as it should. She took the lifter and—prised off the lid, and then uttered an exclamation of vexation.

She had been in such a hurry to put in the two sticks of wood before she milked, that they had jammed together at the top of the fire-box and the embers had burnt themselves out without setting them alight.

It was a mere trifle such as frequently happened when you were in a hurry, but the momentary upset to her plans for—a speedy supper banished her incipient cheerfulness. Somehow it seemed to her ill-omened, and made her feel nervous again. It was different when you were all alone in a blizzard. The ordinary things were not as easy to do as when someone else was there to keep you company.

The house shook to its foundations with each gust. She could feel the cold being blown through the walls into the room as though it were something alive and menacing. The cold had taken all the moisture with which the steam from her kettles had filled the air earlier in the day and frozen it on the inside of the windows. They were covered with an opaque thickness of ice in a formation almost like the scales of a fish.

It was nearly dark, but she was so cold that she could not wait to light the lamp. She took the two pieces of wood out of the fire-box, and, snatching a newspaper from a chair, laid her fire anew. She used plenty of kindling, for she had to have the fire in a hurry.

At last it was ready! She pulled off her mittens, hurting her skinned fingers, took the box of matches from the dresser and struck one of them. Soon she would be warm and be able to attend to her hand. She shivered nervously when she found that the match had no head.

It was a second portent of ill-omen. She glanced round the darkening room with a little quiver of fear. Everything seemed vaguely hostile in that bitter cold, and the very familiarity of the room only served to emphasize her loneliness.

There was only one more match in the box. Her hands were so numb with the cold that she could scarcely hold it, and her injured fingers were torture. She trembled, partly from nervousness and partly from cold, as she struck it.

Just as it flared into light there was a tremendous gust of wind, which blew into the room through the crack under the door and through the very walls, where the boards had contracted from the dryness of the cold. She was afraid that the draught would put out the flame, and as soon as the edge of the paper had caught alight she slammed the door of the firebox with her elbow. She was taking good care not to touch any more metal with her fingers.

She had no fear that the fire would not go this time. Canadian stoves are far superior to an English range, and there is never any difficulty in getting the fire to go if you lay it properly, especially in zero weather. She thought no more about it, and hurried to the dresser to put some cold cream on her fingers. They were hurting so much that she felt it wiser to dress them before lighting the lamp.

The cream eased the pain a little, and she went back to the stove to see how the fire was going. Strange. There was not the roar from the stove pipe that there should have been in such weather. Once more she felt a quiver of fear. It was positively eerie the way everything was going wrong. If only her husband had been there to chaff her for taking such a long time! At the thought of it she felt sick with loneliness.

She put on her right mitten and opened the fire-box. As she had feared, the fire had not caught. It must be bewitched, she thought, for she had laid it properly and the wood was dry enough in all conscience. There was not a vestige of moisture within hundreds of miles in that blizzard. It must be another portent of ill-omen, and in her tension she felt that the fates must indeed be against her.

She took out the sticks of wood and the kindling and straightway understood. The paper itself had not burnt. She held it up to the remnants of the daylight, and once more uttered an exclamation of anger. It was just possible to make out the heading, 'The Sunday Times'.

The paper which her husband's English relations sent to them every week. A good solid paper, she knew, but not the least bit of use for lighting the fire. No English papers seemed to be much good for that purpose, and from past experience she knew that *The Sunday Times* was easily the worst of the lot.

She bit her lip with vexation. It really did seem as if the fates were against her, or was it just because she was alone? Again she glanced fearfully round the room. It was horrible to be alone like that. Why on earth had not she taken a bit more care and used a Canadian paper? There were the *Winnipeg Free Press* and the *Family Herald* on the table. If only she had used them, she would have been warm by this time.

She flung the offending *The Sunday Times* into the wood box, stuffed some pages of the *Family Herald* into the stove and once more set her fire. Now for another box of matches and then at last she would be warm.

But her groping fingers found no matches on their accustomed shelf. Growing more nervously excited every minute, she moved her hand over every inch of that shelf. Then over the one below it. And then over the one above it. She was gasping a little now; for though her fingers encountered cups and plates, bottles of essences and tins of salt and pepper, and all the other appliances of the kitchen, they did not close round the familiar box of matches.

She gave a little cry of alarm, for it did seem as if the place were bewitched and that something dreadful was going to happen to her. It was horrible to be so alone. Just when she thought she was going to have hysterics, she suddenly remembered, and laughed aloud from sheer relief.

Of course! What an idiot she was! It was simply absurd the way your nerves played tricks with you when you were alone.

Her husband had taken the other three boxes with him for his stay in the shack. She sighed with relief when she remembered how they had laughed over it that very morning when he put them in his pocket just before he left. How he had said it was a good thing she did not smoke, or else he could only have taken two boxes with him, and that she must not forget to buy a packet in Sunset that afternoon.

Of course, everything had a rational explanation if you did not get rattled and started thinking the house was bewitched just because you were alone. And she had bought a packet of matches in Sunset. You did not forget things like that when you only went shopping once in a blue moon and if there was enough butter made to trade with the store. She laughed once more as she stepped to the table where the box of groceries was lying. All she had to do was to open the packet, take out a box of matches, strike one and then all would be well. The stove would get red-hot, and the whole house would be warm, and she could laugh at the blizzard raging outside.

But when her hands rummaged among the paper parcels in the box they did not feel a packet of matches. Thinking it must be because of her mittens, she took them off. She shivered as her bare fingers touched the snow between the parcels. She felt each one deliberately, expecting each time she touched one to find it was the packet she wanted.

Her heart thumped with excitement and fear when she came to the end of the box and still she had not found the packet. The house must be bewitched after all, or else she would have found it by this time. For a moment she stood in irresolution, and then, sobbing with anxiety, she turned the box upside down on the table and blew the snow away from the parcels.

It was dark and she could only see a blurred outline where they rested. She wanted to snatch at them in her search, but she knew she must be calm or she really would have hysterics. The loneliness was more terrifying than ever now, and the blizzard seemed to be threatening to carry away the whole house. She bit her lip and forced herself to stand still until she had got her nerves under control once more.

After a minute's wait she sat on a chair, put the box in her lap and methodically picked up each parcel one by one from the table and laid it in the box. Her heart began to thump again as she was nearing the end and still she could not find that packet.

At last there were no more parcels on the table, and the matches were not there! At first she could not believe it, and moved her arms backwards and forwards over the table in ever wider sweeps, until finally she knocked two plates on the far side on to the floor. Then she was forced to believe. She was alone and she had no matches. It was dark and she would not get warm now.

It must have been the packet of matches the wind had blown away when she said good-bye to Mawson. Why, oh why, had not she stopped to look? They were past finding now. Why had not she taken more care when she set the fire? Why had not she lit the lamp first? Why...?

Her nerves got the better of her, and she screamed with terror. She was experienced enough to understand her plight. She knew that she would certainly freeze to death before morning if she went to sleep, and was more than likely to do so even if she kept herself awake. She had been on the move from two that morning getting things ready for her husband's early start, and after that making butter to trade for their groceries, seeing to the stock, and then going to Sunset. She had eaten nothing since eleven, she was dog-tired and ravenously hungry, and above all else she was cold—cold right inside to the innermost part of her body. She did not know if she could keep awake till morning, and, even if she did, the blizzard was very unlikely to have died down.

It was hopeless to think of trying to reach her neighbours. Along the straight prairie roads she would never find her way in that maelstrom of whirling snow. And if she could find her way, she would probably die of cold before she had gone a mile. And there was nothing in the house to warm her.

Ah! She straightened with a faint hope as she thought of the barn. If she could reach it, she could snuggle between the two cows and perhaps keep life in her that way. She half started up from her chair and then sank down again despondently. There was not the slightest hope of her being able to reach the barn without a lantern.

She knew that even with lanterns, and warmed after a good meal, men had gone out in a blizzard to attend to their stock and never been seen alive again: had just set out to walk the fifty or hundred yards which they walked four times every day of their lives, and had missed their way in that bewildering fury of powdered snow. There was nothing for her to do except walk up and down the room and try to keep awake till morning came.

The loneliness, and the darkness, and the cold, weighed upon her like tangible enemies. It was so dark that she blundered into the wall at the far end of the room, and her head bumped into something. Her nerves almost made her jump from it, but when she put out her hand she felt a familiar outline and her stifled cry turned into an exclamation of joy.

The telephone! Why had not she thought of it before? Even in that awful storm, when her plight was known, somehow or other they would form an expedition in Sunset and bring help to her.

But as she turned the handle to ring up Central her joy gave way once more to despair, all the more bitter for the momentary ray of hope. As if she could not have remembered! The telephone had been disconnected months ago, because they could not afford the expense, and the telephone company had not bothered to take the instrument away. When No. 1 Northern was only sixty cents a bushel—in Winnipeg, the telephone company would not be asked to install it anywhere else. They had more disconnected instruments than they could handle as it was.

With a sigh of utter despair she pulled her overcoat closer round her shoulders and resumed her walk. Fifteen paces to the door and fifteen paces back to the telephone. Back and forward. Back and forward, and all the time her brain flayed by the tortures of Tantalus.

She was cold, and she knew that there was a great pile of wood in the box by the stove; she was hungry, and she knew that there was bread and butter and jam and pork and veal in plenty; she was afraid of the dark, and there was a lamp on the table filled with coal oil; she was lonely, and there was a telephone. But none of these things was any good to her, and as she paced slowly up and down she found herself babbling incoherently: 'Water, water everywhere, nor any drop to drink.'

Her woollen blizzard-cap was stiff against her face where her breath had frozen, and her injured fingers were throbbing. Before her eyes swam visions of a red-hot stove and a hot supper on the table and a light in the lamp, until she could stand them no longer. Even though she knew it to be useless she simply had to do something different.

If only she were not so hungry! She stumbled to the pantry and automatically caught up the bread tin. With trembling fingers she opened it and took out a loaf. She found a knife and tried to cut a slice, but it would not make the slightest impression. The loaf was frozen as hard as a stone.

'Ask for bread and ye give them a stone.' The words danced before her eyes until she knew she was nearly hysterical again. She ran her hand aimlessly along the shelf until it encountered a pat of butter. That alone out of all her supply of food would not be frozen like a stone. She gouged out a lump from the pat with her knife and had almost put it to her lips when she remembered her hurt fingers. If the knife touched her lips it would take all the skin off them.

She stuck the lump on her mittens and bit off a piece, but, famished as she was, it was so greasy that it nearly made her sick. She moaned with despair and idly ran her hand along the shelf again. It encountered a long, round object, and for a moment she could not think what it was. Her half-frozen fingers in their clumsy mittens could not feel, and she fidgeted with it until with a shock of surprise she saw a ray of light.

She was holding the electric torch they had bought in case they had a breakdown in their car when driving at night, and it had been put on the shelf when they could no longer afford the car. Not much good to her now, but the light was a little bit of company.

She returned to the kitchen and flashed it over the room. The walls and roof of the house cracked at intervals almost like a pistol shot as the timber contracted. She did not like the colour of the little bit of her cheek showing in the opening of her blizzard-cap. It was a dirty white and she knew she had a touch of frostbite there.

She must do something! Her despairing brain caught at the hope that there might be an odd match lying somewhere. She knew it was hopeless, but any sort of action was better than aimless pacing up and down. With the aid of her torch she searched every nook and cranny of the house, but there was no match. She turned out the drawers and all the pockets of her husband's clothes.

How she wished that she had not lectured him on his habit of leaving loose matches in his pockets, in case they set the house on fire; and how she wished he had remained firm in his contention that there was no danger in that! If only he had gone on laughing at her, and had not conquered his habit simply to please her and turned out his pockets every time he took off his clothes!

She closed the last drawer and returned to the kitchen to resume her walk. Up and down. Back and forward. Till her brain was mesmerized and her legs ached with fatigue and cold. She was so tired that she could keep going no longer.

At any cost she must sit down and rest for a little while. She found her chair and sat down. Her head began to nod and her eyes closed, but she fought against the temptation. That way led to certain death. She began to count the minutes to help herself keep awake, but once more her eyes closed. She tried desperately to think of some possible place she might have overlooked in her search for an odd match, some possible garment of her husband's which perhaps she had missed.

Her brain swam with visions of overalls and pairs of trousers. She could not think of one she had missed, and they made her dizzy like the sheep she counted when she lay awake at night sometimes. Her head nodded off again, and this time she did fall into a doze.

The electric torch slid from her nerveless fingers on to the floor, and the bang awoke her with a start. If it had not been for that torch she would soon have been dead. Thoroughly frightened at her near escape, she picked it up and once more began her walk. But the brief period of sleep had given her subconscious mind a chance to work, and suddenly she remembered.

There was an old pair of blue denim overalls hanging on a nail on the veranda wall. They had been there for over a year. She had been meaning to cut them up for cloths to wash the milk pails with and was always forgetting. There was just one chance in a million that he left them there before he had started to turn out his pockets.

One chance in a million. There might be a match in them. Anyway she would see, and then if there was not she might just as well walk towards the barn and the warmth of the cows' bodies. She would never reach them, but it was better to die quickly attempting something than to die slowly trying to keep awake in the kitchen.

With her breath coming in sobs she went to the door. There was a pile of snow where it had drifted through the key-hole. She caught hold of the door handle and began to turn it. But before she opened the door she glanced back and looked round the darkened room in which she had toiled and eaten and, in spite of the drudgery, been happy with her husband. She knew that it was a thousand to one she would never see it again.

With an effort she tore her eyes away and pushed open the door. It slammed behind her as the wind and snow swooped down like a million knives cutting at her body. She flashed her torch along the veranda wall. The beam of light wavered and then fastened on a tattered pair of blue overalls. There was still a chance!

She crept towards them and pulled off her right mitten with her teeth. Surely after all the misfortunes of the last few hours it was too much to expect him to have left any matches in the pockets. And if he had, supposing the pockets had holes in them. And if....

She had no more time to think, for her fingers were inside the first pocket. As she had feared, it was empty. She sobbed as she tried the second—and then the third. They, too, were empty.

She drew in her breath and paused. There was only one more pocket—the right hip-pocket—and she could not bring herself to try it. If it was empty too, then she was done for.

She could hardly move her bare fingers and knew that if she waited another minute or two they would be frostbitten. There was nothing for it but to try, and then, if she drew a blank, that last walk to the barn. With the impatience of desperation she thrust her fingers in the pocket. They felt nothing, and with a gasp of despair she was about to withdraw them when they touched a little hard object in one corner.

It was scarcely worth trying, but she picked at it with the nail of her forefinger. It seemed to be round, and she caught her breath with excitement and fear. She was sure now that it was the head of a match, but her fingers were so cold, and she trembled so in her eagerness, that for a moment she could not move it.

Finally her reawakening hope gave her the wit to push the torch underneath the outside of the pocket. She clawed and picked at the object with her nail, and then at last she knew that it was a match, a whole match which had slipped down a tiny hole in the pocket.

Slowly and with infinite care she drew it upward with her fingernail while the torch in her left hand held the cloth steady. Higher and higher it came until at last she was able to close the other fingers of her right hand round it. She cried aloud with joy as she clutched it, and her head swam from the reaction. She stood thus trying to pull herself together, for she had yet to regain the kitchen and light the match. Her hand was almost useless from the cold, and if she was not careful she would drop the match as she took it out of the pocket.

Salvation was so near, and yet it was so fatally easy to make a mistake. With infinite caution she put her mouth against the overalls and slowly drew her lips away from the mitten she had been holding in her teeth. She pressed her cheek against the end of it to keep it against the overalls and then slowly edged her lips into the pocket.

In her excitement she almost bit the match in two as her teeth closed over it, but with a great effort she restrained herself and at last stood erect with the end of it in her mouth. Her right hand felt dead as she wriggled it into her mitten again, but the match was still between her teeth as she turned and made for the door.

She had won, and the knowledge made her calm and confident in her purpose. She knew what she had to deal with, and this time she would not fail. While she stumbled the three yards to the door her brain reviewed what she must do.

She must find the match-box she had dropped on the floor and then open the door of the fire-box, sprinkle a little coal oil from the bottle in the pantry on the wood just in case of accident; and when she had done that, and not before, she could take off her right mitten. She had just enough feeling left in her right hand to strike that one match, and after that she would have to rub snow on it to guard against frostbite. And after that on her face, and then after that light the heater and fasten up her other hand, and chop the frozen milk and water out of the buckets with the little bench axe by the wood box, and then...

With the match between her teeth she opened the door and once more stood in the kitchen. It no longer seemed hostile, and she no longer feared the loneliness, for now she had hope and something definite to do. Her head was clear and she knew that she would not fail as she switched on the torch, which was beginning to wane but ought to last until she had lighted the lamp.

The match-box was covered with snow dropped from her coat, but it was so powdery that she blew it off with one puff through her clenched teeth. Her hand did not shake until she had opened the door of the fire-box and sprinkled the coal oil over the wood.

But when she had wriggled out of her right mitten and knelt down on the floor by the fire-box, she had to work her fingers like a pianist before she could trust them to take the match from her teeth. Gingerly she transferred the match to her fingers, propped the torch up against the leg of the stove, and then took the match-box from the top, where she had laid it.

Now that the crucial moment had come she was nervous again. She was afraid to look round. Her brain told her there was no other preparation to make, but it took her a terrible, seemingly endless minute before she could bring herself to make the final move. Her life depended on that match, and if she failed...

But she would not fail. With an unconscious gesture of defiance against fate she held the match-box inside the fire-box with her left hand right up against the paper, forced her deadened right hand slowly and carefully inside the opening, and with drawn breath struck the match.

The paper, sodden with coal oil, burst into flame which scorched her left mitten and made her frozen right hand throb with pain, but she scarcely noticed it.

The fire roared up the chimney in a deafening crescendo, and she shut the door of the fire-box with a gasp of ecstasy.

Soon she would be warm.

THE HAUNTS OF ISABELINE

C.H. Donald

I

It has been a severe winter in the Himalayas, and an early one, but once more the sun shines bright and warm, and green patches of grass here and there, in a great wilderness of dazzling white snow, acknowledge its power and the advent of spring. A flock of lighthearted little choughs circling in the bright blue sky above sing to each other, and convey the joyful tidings to all whom they may concern, that the snow is fast melting from their feeding grounds, and that it is high time to be out and enjoying life in such glorious weather.

Isabeline, the little brown mother bear, hears the call, and pokes her nose out of her hollow at the root of an ancient mountain oak, where she has spent the winter, and given birth to two tiny wee cubs. The nose is followed by a great shaggy head and two little beads of eyes, blinking hard in the glare, roll in their sockets, while her nose wobbles about from side to side, to ascertain from every passing zephyr of the presence of any lurking enemy. Her keen scent, however, tells her that all is well, and that she may leave her two woolly balls and come out. Stealthily a great paw, armed with large white nails, next makes an appearance, and then the whole bear in all her glory of a magnificent winter coat, steps out into the sun, to stretch her weary limbs after her long winter sleep. She can still hear the cry of the choughs far, far above her, as she looks up the valley to the alpine pastures which she knows so well, and slowly she moves off in that direction, her legs so stiff that they have some difficulty in bearing her weight, but at each step they get better, and soon 'Isabeline' is well above the forests and revelling in the warm sun.

There is, however, no time for enjoyment and the pangs of hunger must be first attended to, before she hurries back to the little ones in the cave. The sight that meets her eyes on everyside is not very reassuring and there does not seem very much prospect of satisfying her ravenous appetite on these snow-covered slopes, but she sees the little green path and makes for it and is rewarded for her pains by getting a few mouthfulls of luscious young, wild carrot tops, as *hors d'oeuvre*. Thence she slowly makes her way down again, turning over all the big stones she passes and getting from under one, a nest of beetles or ant's larvae, and under the next a few blades of sprouting grasses, till eventually she finds herself in a ravine, from the side of which all the snow has been blown off by the wind and the grass coming up sweet and green everywhere, and here she makes up for lost time. As she feeds on she becomes aware that she is not the first of her kind that has visited this spot during that morning, and her nose tells her that another has gone over the same ground, only a few hours before her, but there is no time to think of others, as she goes from tuft to tuft, and here and there turns over a stone to see if it conceals anything edible, beneath it.

She is not nearly satisfied, but the sun is high up in the horizon, and it's time that she made her way back to the little ones at home, as it is not safe to wander about at a time when her arch enemy, man, may be about. Day after day she might be seen grazing on the bare plateaux, in the early mornings, and late evenings, and as the snow melts, new pastures come into being, and she has much less difficulty in satisfying her cravings than she formerly had.

Spring has past into summer, and the snow has given place to green fields of grass and flowers of every hue. Masses of dainty primulae, king-cups and anenomes, clothe the plateaux on every side in gay pinks, yellows and purples, whilst a bright patch of blue tells of a bed of little forget-me-nots or gentians, and there on that crag, all by itself, too proud to mix with the rest, waves gently in the breeze, the gem of the mountains, in its wonderful electric blue, the blue mountain poppy.

The little cubs have been all over these hills with their mother, since we last saw her, and though only three months old now, are fine sturdy little specimens, and up to every kind of mischief their ursine brains can devise. In size there is practically no difference between them, and in colour they are identical, except that the one has a small white waist-coat which is almost indistinguishable in the other. In temperament however, they are as the poles apart, and if you could only get near enough to see the wee, restive little beady eyes of each, you could have no doubt as to which had the wits of the family.

I had seen old Isabeline on the very first occasion that she had ventured out of her hollow in the tree, and I had from afar, coveted that glossy, light brown winter coat of hers, which I had examined carefully through my glasses, and as she approached the green patch in the snow, she little guessed, poor little lady, how near she was to feeling a rifle bullet smashing through her bones. I, too, had seen the green patch and knew she would go to it, so keeping the spur of the hill between us, had reached a point a few yards above it, just before her, and watched her as she grazed. I had seen that beautiful coat, but I had also seen something else, when she came to within 30 yards of me, which the glasses had not revealed, and which proved her salvation.

This was the lack of hair, in patches, underneath, which showed me that she was the mother of one, if not two little babies which eagerly waited for her arrival, and would starve in their cave if some cruel hand laid her low now. From that date on she became my especial care, and many and many is the time, that I have sat and watched her turning over the boulders and grazing on the grassy slopes, little dreaming how near she was to her enemy, who, for the time being, was also her friend. When 'Devil' and 'Fool', as I christened the cubs, first made their appearance in public, early in June, I had the good fortune to meet them at very close quarters, without their knowing it, and from that hour fell in love with them, and was determined to have them for my own, but how to get them, without shooting the mother, was another matter altogether. However, there was no hurry and I could afford to wait and watch, and before long got to recognise the one from the other almost as well as the mother could have done. There was something in the Devil's eyes and general saucy devil-may-care look that was quite wanting in poor Fool. It was not only in his eyes but in his general demeanour, for it was not necessary to be near him to be able to recognise him, he was unmistakable 40 yards away.

What it was, I could not tell, but it was there, and if anyone who had never seen the cubs before, had been asked which was Devil and which Fool he would have pointed them out correctly, the very first shot.

One evening I had gone up for a quiet stroll to Isabeline's

haunts; it was a warm afternoon and very still, even at this altitude, and whilst waiting under a rock, I had got drowsy and fallen asleep.

I woke up with a start hearing strange noises somewhere very near, and there to my delight, not ten yards away, embracing each other, were Devil and Fool. Such a time as they were having, on the soft turf, and the mother a few yards below, not taking the least notice of her dear little hopefuls' gambol. This was luck, the wind blew directly from them to me, so there was no possibility of my being winded, and until it changed, or they got above me, I would be able to feast my eyes on their delightful antics. The fond embrace in which I first saw them, culminated in the Fool losing his balance and toppling over with the Devil still holding on to him, and down they went rolling in a ball for a few yards, when Devil loosened his hold, and ran for his mother. Right under her legs he rushed, and then turning round, stood up on his hind legs, with his forepaws on her back, and coyly peeped at Fool from this coign of vantage. I just suppressed a loud laugh, for anything more grotesque than the Devil's rolling eyes and twitching snout, and the poor Fool's tired look and perplexity, would be hard to find. After a couple of seconds or so, Fool too made a rush for his mother's legs, evidently hoping to get a grip of Devil from below, but Devil had played this game before, seemingly, and was prepared, for as soon as Fool emerged on the other side, Devil fell on his back, with both paws firmly gripping Fool's sides and his teeth in Fool's neck, and thus got quite a pleasant little ride at, Fool's expense, till his weight brought Fool down on his nose. Up got Devil again, and made for his mother, and Fool, picking himself up, quietly set about following his mother's example and feeding. The Devil, though, was irrepressible, and, not finding

Fool sociably inclined, he looked at his mother as much as to say 'shall I?' and began tearing up the ground with his forefeet, and backing at the same time, then suddenly made a plunge at her, but evidently rather misjudged his distance, for he landed right on her head, which had the effect of jabbing her snout rather violently into the ground. Next instant old Devil was flying through space as though out of a gun barrel, and landed on his back quite 10 feet down the hill. The mother went on with her grazing and took no further interest but the Devil's face was a treat. He stood up and looked at his mother out of the corner of his eye, and such a look!

I am sure that had he been able to speak English, the words he would have muttered would have been 'nasty old cat'. He could not have expressed himself more plainly than he did, though.

Now this would probably have kept Devil quiet for some time, and made him think of more serious things, but just then he looked up and his eye met Fool's, in which he plainly saw written the words 'that served you jolly well right', and that coming from Fool was not to be endured at any price, so he made a savage charge at him, and once again I saw them in a loving embrace, but this time they had both got a good deal to say to each other as they rolled down, locked in each other's arms, and from the way it was all said, I knew it was nasty names that they were calling each other. A depression in the ground hid them from my view for a few seconds, and what was my surprise to suddenly hear the angry 'unf unf unf' half sneeze, half grunt of a bear alarmed, and angry. Up went the mother's head in a second, with her nose held well to the wind, and giving vent to a deeper 'unf unf unf' than the last I had heard, off she went, after Devil and Fool, but pulled up at the top of the depression, where I could still see her, with all the long hair on her withers bristling with anger, at something I could not see. The babies had both now joined their mother and all there stood looking down at, to me, the unknown disturber of their peace.

What could it be? Not a man, for they would not stand there looking at him, and besides, there were no shepherds on this plateau as yet, and nobody but a shepherd would come here. I began to get as excited as the bears were, but could not move from my rock without attracting the attention of one or the other of the three before me, so had to curb my impatience and sit where I was, but was soon rewarded, for the mother gradually edged off and down into the depression and both the cubs followed. I was out of my hiding at once, and taking advantage of a small spur behind one got quickly round it.

As my head got over the rising ground, the breeze brought up the shrill 'chick chick' constantly repeated notes of the monaul pheasant, this also was his note of alarm and warning, but far down in the valley.

With my glasses I searched every inch of the rolling plateaux before me and below me, but not a thing could I see anywhere, and yet I felt certain that something was astir somewhere, what could it be?

Just as I was getting tired of looking at nothing, a movement a long way down the hill caught my eye, but look as I would nothing could I make of it, though I gazed again and again with a powerful pair of Zeiss glasses, at the exact spot where I had seen the movement with the naked eye. Looking still lower down, I suddenly spotted a fox digging for voles some 200 yards below where I had first seen the 'movement'.

This would account for the cry of alarm of the monaul, but did not in the least explain the uneasiness of the bears, or that movement I saw. Still worried, I kept on looking at the fox, a tiny speck in the distance, when again that movement caught my eye, and much more distinct this time. Again I got the glasses out and looked and looked till my eyes ached, but nothing was visible, and yet I was sure that I was not mistaken. More puzzled than ever, I decided to watch the country around the fox for a few minutes, and before a couple of minutes had gone I distinctly saw a greyish object flash through the air and again disappear into the very bowels of the earth. Again my glasses revealed nothing, for some time, but at length, on a grey boulder, I noticed the twitch of a tail, and there right before me, was a beautiful panther crouching low on the rock. I must have had my eyes and glasses on him over and over again, and yet not seen him, and now that I had seen him, he was as plain almost as the bears had been a few minutes previously. It was absurd to risk a 400 yards long shot, but how was I to get nearer in such open country, was the question? But then again why those sudden movements on his part and why was he now crouching on that rock?

Then a thought struck me. He was stalking the fox. If so, that would be something worth watching, and I soon forgot all about Isabeline and her family and settled myself to watch developments in this direction, For five full minutes that panther sat immovable as the rock on which he crouched, and then without a moment's warning or the slightest movement of a muscle, he sprang straight into the air and stopped dead on a rock some ten feet lower down, in the identical position in which he left the last rock. I looked at the fox but she had noticed nothing, and was moving leisurely about in quest of her voles. The next move of the panther was different, and he sprang lightly off the rock and crouching low, went very stealthily yet with quick steps, down the hill. This time the fox looked up, and immediately the panther crouched and lay still. The fox, however, like me, had got a glimpse of something and though not scared, was still suspicious and kept looking up every few seconds, but the panther never moved a muscle, and only about 80 to 100 yards divided them.

Gazing through binoculars for any length of time is very tiring for the eyes, and though loth to miss a single state of the drama before me, I put them down till the feline should again make a move, keeping my eyes on him in the meantime. It was about ten minutes ere he moved again and this time covered a good twenty paces ere he stopped, but the fox too was changing her ground and still kept her distance. She was now no longer straight below him as she had been when I first saw him, but had got several yards to one side, yet he still went on straight down.

Could he have lost sight of her, and is he making for the place he last saw her in, from the rock, in the fond hope that she is still there? Not much fear of his taking those all—seeing eyes of his off her for a single second. I soon saw his little game; there was a huge rock some 30 feet to the rear of the fox and he meant to get that between him and her as soon as possible. A slight pause of a few seconds and as the fox did not look up, he moved stealthily forward and got on to a rock and very slowly peered over. The little fox still merrily went from hole to hole, noising each, oblivious of all danger, and as she turned her back for a second, I saw a sight I shall never forget.

The panther had been looking over the rock at the time, with his fore paws resting on it and his hind feet on the ground below, and yet from that non-jumping attitude, he sprang clear 20 feet or so down, and looked for all the world like a shooting star. This spring and a rush and he was behind the coveted rock, but what in the meantime had alarmed the fox? She was not looking in his direction, but rather down the hill and below him yet 'pheaw pheaw-aw-aw' came her long warning cry.

I could no longer see the panther now, but knew he was only waiting for the fox to turn her head, and she was as good as dead, and then, perhaps I might have a chance of a stalk after him. The fox looks this way and that, undoubtedly alarmed, but unaware of the cause of it. Some wonderful instinct warning her to be on her guard, for what else could it be that alarmed her? Had it been some sound the feline made, or had she got his scent, she would have run off some distance away from either, before turning to 'pheaw,' but it is something in no way located, yet she is aware in some vague way of the presence of danger.

It comes too; as she turns her head there is a mighty rush, and a something with the speed of a falcon is on her, almost before she has time to look back, but there again, that something has befriended her, and with a sudden whisk of her tail, and a twist that my eye could not even follow, she has evaded those relentless talons, and somehow doubled under the panther's legs and is flying for life down the hill, to find cover in the birch jungle below. Strangely enough the panther never even attempted to follow, but accepted his defeat, and sat down on a rock and watched the fox racing down the hill. I could hear the 'pheaws' coming up from the forest below, for a long time after.

I carefully changed my position and getting into a dip of the hill crawled round till I got a ridge in between myself and the feline, and then ran as hard as I could for a spot I marked out in my mind as being within 100 yards of him, and arriving there, stalked very carefully over, till I could get my eyes just over the top, but he was 'non est'.

High and low I searched, but not a sign of him could I

find and as night was fast approaching, I had to make my way back to camp, and leave him.

II

In the meantime, while I interested myself in the panther and his doings, Isabeline and her cubs had wandered out of sight, and I saw them no more for some time to come. I had rather wondered at the bears giving their note of alarm for a panther, and I do not suppose that a solitary one would have bothered his head much about him one way or the other, but with a mother with tiny cubs, it is different, as Mr Spots would not hesitate long about making a meal off a cub if he got the chance, and Isabeline had long ago taught Devil and Fool to be careful of his scent, and warn her at once should they come across it.

I have already said that I had wanted to capture the cubs and have them as pets, but one cannot go and shoot an animal one has taken an interest in for over a month, in cold blood, though I have no doubt, had I seen her with the cubs the first time she came out, I should not have thought twice about it. The next time I came across them, the summer had given place to late autumn, the sheep had left the alpine pastures, the flowers had bowed their heads to the cutting winds, and the glorious verdant carpets on which Devil and Fool had been wont to play had assumed a sombre brown. In the valley below, the birch and maples had clothed themselves in their golden tints, and lower still could be seen the brilliant scarlet of the Virginian creeper clustering about the dark green of the spruce and silver-fir.

The scene in all its wonderful variety of colours, even though it lacked the vivid greens of spring, defied description. Above, the grand old giants reared their virgin snow-capped peaks into the clear blue sky, and in the gorge, just below that mighty peak, a glacier grim, glistened with blues and greens as the rays of the morning sun touched it.

Well might Isabeline be proud of her lovely haunts, and loth to leave them till the bleak winter winds and hard frosts which made digging impossible, drove her down to more sheltered nooks. The hardy 'bhurrel', the blue sheep of the Himalayas can alone face those icy blasts, and appears to revel in the blizzards that howl round his inhospitable, rugged peaks.

As soon as the frost sets in, and even Isabeline's great claws and forearm can make no impression on the hard ground, she thinks of looking about for a sequestered home in which to spend the winter. A cave beneath an overhanging rock, or the hollow at the root of a tree, which will keep her warm and dry and yet permit the passage of fresh air, are selected with much care, for her long winter sleep. She will enter it a fat tubby ball, almost round, and issue four to five months later, simply skin and bone, but the possessor of a lovely coat.

It was in late October, when I came across Isabeline and her cubs. The latter were now well-grown, and to catch them would have been no easy matter, so I was obliged to give up all thought of it, but my interest in them had not abated in the slightest and I was as ready as ever to watch them at their play. Determined to find out their hibernating quarters, I used to be up on their feeding grounds before the sun touched them and on the first occasion contented myself by watching them leave for the trees, as the day advanced, through my glasses. But that proved a fruitless watch, as I lost sight of them as soon as they got into the forest.

The next time, some ten days later, I decided to follow them, but the ground being caked and hard with frost, I had the greatest difficulty in seeing their tracks, and lost them entirely in the forest, where they went over a succession of rocks and boulders. The following week a light fall of snow came to my help, and the morning after it, I made my way up to her favourite ravine and was just in time to see her and the cubs disappearing into some birch jungle. There was no mistaking their tracks now, and on hands and knees I crawled after them among the dense tangle of branches which being bent down year after year by the winter snows, grow down instead of standing up straight.

Careful not to get too near or disturb them in any way, I carefully avoided each branch, either stepping over or crawling under it. Thus I must have covered over a mile, and was thankful to find myself getting into more open cover, the birch giving place to oak and pine. All this time I had not got a single glimpse of them, though I know from the tracks that I was very near. Under one tree I found marks of the mother's claws, where she had raked up some twigs and branches, preparatory to lying down for the day, but had changed her mind and moved on. This at all events meant that she would not go very much further and it behoved me to be all the more careful, in case I stumbled on to her unawares from below, in which case she might charge and tend to make things nasty, in defence of her cubs.

I had my trusty rifle with me, but there are times when it is difficult to be quick enough with it, and this might be one of them. Carefully, with one eye on the tracks and the other on the ground ahead, I plodded on, removing every twig that chanced in my way, and to my joy I at last came to where the tracks began moving downhill. This gave me a much better command of the position and also enabled me to see further. A bear, brown or black, if he selects a tree to sit behind, will almost invariably sit on the upper side and not below it, so

I should now have a chance of seeing the family from some distance if they meant to sleep under a tree and not go into a cave, which at this season, however, was unlikely.

On the other hand, this would not help me to find, their hibernating quarters, but having come so far, I intended to continue now, wherever they went, and follow them. A tragopan gave me the first intimation of their exact whereabouts, for not 50 yards ahead, I could hear his plaintive cry as, disturbed by their approach, he rushed up the hill uttering his curious single note. This meant that I could hurry on for a few paces, as a spur divided us, and any noise I made would not reach them, but I must be careful, not to frighten the tragopan unduly and make him fly, as that might put the bears on the qui vive.

The bears had not wasted their time while seeking their place for the mid-day siesta, as over-turned stones and logs of wood testified, and in one place I had to make a dive into some undergrowth to avoid a nest of angry jungle wasps, whose home had been ruthlessly torn out and their winter store of honey robbed by the furry marauders ahead.

A musk-deer near whose lair they passed, stood up and gave his cry of alarm—'fitch fitch'—at intervals of a few seconds, and so engaged was he in looking at the bears, that I got to within 30 feet of him, and could see his gleaming white tushes and saw him stamp his foot, as he 'fitched' and wagged his little scut.

One ear was held forward and the other twitching back and fro, alive to every sound. I crouched behind a stump and very gently 'fitched' in return. In a second his head turned in my direction, and he stood staring intently, not being able to make it out, the very embodiment of grace and daintiness. I dare not alarm him or he might go racing off down the hill in his succession of jumps, a mode of locomotion, peculiar to the little beasts, and yet I must get him away from here, before I could move myself, and in the meantime, the bears were getting further and further away. 'Fitch fitch' I said to him and 'fitch sh sh' was his reply, and a violent stamp on the ground. A second 'fitch' from me was too much for his nerves and had the desired effect. With half a dozen dainty little bounds, all four legs rising and falling at the same time, he fled up the hill and with a final 'fitch' disappeared from view behind some rocks.

Again I moved forward and, climbing a small rise over which the tracks led me, looked down on an expanse of melting snow and at the foot of it saw Devil and Fool playing hide and seek. Glancing at the tracks, I could see that they had not troubled to walk down, but had simply glissaded or rolled the whole way to the bottom. Even Isabeline had become playful after her slide, for, as one of the cubs ran round her, she got up on her hind legs, her great fat forearms swaying from side to side, and gave vent to a loud snort ending up with a tremendous puff as though blowing bubbles.

Little Fool rushed up and also got on to his hind legs in front of her, and the pair promptly set to work to do a little boxing, but Devil did not see why he should be left out in the cold, and made for poor Fool. A fair spar, with the mother as umpire, ensued, but as usual it did not last long and ended up in close grips and a roll in the snow. Devil's honour was satisfied and once more the trio started off up the opposite hill, and I had to sit where I was till they went round the next spur, and once more took up the trail from the next ridge.

I had been most fortunate all this time in having the wind blowing down hill, but it was now time for it to change. In the Himalayas the wind usually blows down the valleys from four or five o'clock in the afternoon till 8 or 9 a.m. the following morning, and uphill for the rest of the day, but this fact would not trouble me so long as the bears kept to the contour of the hills, but if they suddenly went down a valley I should be discovered at once if I attempted to follow, so in that case I would have to wait till they had climbed up the other side.

As I topped the crest I found before me a ravine covered with a forest of spruce and silver-fir, and now left convinced that this was the place the bears had been making for, and would now lie up under some old forest giant. Nor was I wrong. Just below me was the tree they had selected for their seista the previous day, but now they had gone down lower, and I must be cautious as they might come to a halt any moment. I crawled along a few paces and was pulled up sort by hearing a twig crack, and peeping round the trunk of a tree, I espied Isabeline busy making up a snug bed for herself, and both the cubs interestedly watching operations.

Foiled in my hopes of seeing their winter quarters I took my sandwiches out of my pocket and proceeded to replenish the inner man, and at the same time keep an eye on the bears. Having removed any stones or hard twigs from under her, the old lady sat up on her haunches and had a good look all round, with her nose well to the wind. Satisfied that all was well she thought about attending to her toilet. A great big hind paw began very deliberately scratching the back of her head and, that done, she lay down with both her fore-paws in front of her and surveyed her huge white claws. Devil still had something on his mind and went down a little way to investigate the roots of another tree, but Fool sat down alongside his mother and getting his hind foot into his mouth, was busy for the next ten minutes sucking it, making an extraordinary gurgling the while. Devil too came up and joined the other two, and half an hour from the time they arrived there everyone was sound asleep, bunched close together. Even though I had seen them settle themselves, I could not make out where one began or the other ended. They looked like one great brown stone except for the fact that every now and again a puff of wind stirred the hair on one of their backs. There was nothing now left for me to do, but to get back home, but before doing so, I would give them a chance of winding me, to see if they kept their noses open even in sleep.

Going back over the spur I had just come over, I descended to their level and quietly got some 20 yards below their tree and hid myself behind another. I had not been there many seconds, when a small head looked round the edge, the nose well in the air and working vigorously, and with a low 'unf unf unf' awoke the other two. Both the cubs took to their heels up the hill but the mother waited just long enough to see that nothing followed, and then went after her sons. Their education had not been neglected, evidently, and the mother no doubt was not a little proud of her apt pupils. Had I not seen them go off I might have passed them within a few yards and never known that there was a bear within a mile of me, so quietly had they all disappeared. Fortunately for mother bear, in the higher Himalayas there is so very little that can harm her of her young that she can instruct them pretty thoroughly as to what they should avoid.

'All man's scents are not necessarily dangerous but it is as well to steer clear of them all. That which is tainted with the smell of goat and sheep, or with that of cows and buffaloes, you need not run from, but just get out of his way and get behind a log or a tree till he has passed. If it is pure man's scent, whether he means mischief or not, fly the moment you get it, and keep to thick scrub as long as you can till well out of his reach, and then go over all the stones and rocks you can find to leave no track. If you get the smell of a panther, give me warning, and keep near me. Goats and sheep are very nice eating but do not go too near a flock while it is still light, unless you can find a straggler. Beware of a flock with which there is smell of dog, as they will bark and rouse the camp and guide the men on your scent, and you will have to give up your dinner even if you have had the luck to get it away. You will be a match for any two or three dogs, but you can do nothing when the dogs are followed by half a dozen men armed with big sticks. Buffaloes will do you no harm if you do them none, and though our cousin the black bear has no difficulty in killing them now and again, and we are stronger than he, yet he has got sharp claws with which he can get a firm hold on the back of a buffalo and so hang on till the animal becomes frantic, and falls over a cliff or breaks a leg, but our claws are no good for that sort of thing, being meant only for digging. The same applies to cows and bullocks, though when you are full grown you may be able to manage a cow, but be careful, as sometimes one or two of the bulls with the herd may charge, and in the open, he will get the best of it. A wheat crop is a very pleasant place to spend a night in, but if grazing is good in our own haunts eschew such luxuries, as they are often fraught with danger, and if it is known that we make raids on the crops, man with a gun may be there in hiding to receive you one night. Keep to your own lovely feeding grounds, and follow the instructions I have so often drummed into your heads and you will live to be as old as you desire, but remember that curiosity killed the cat, and will be the end of you, if you are not very careful.'

The advice was good, and though curiosity was Devil's

besetting sin, he was getting over it as he grew up, and after the one or two frights his mother gave him, began to learn that it was enough for him to discover the presence of danger through his nose, without trying to see it as well.

Eighteen months went by, and I had not been able to visit the haunts of Isabeline again, but I had heard of her and the cubs, now grown almost as big as herself, from shepherds and others who had spent the preceding summer near her. Three bears always together, had been frequently reported to me, but no one had ever feared of them attacking sheep, but of late, one huge beast had also taken up his quarters and he had done a good deal of damage among the flocks.

The villagers had begged me to go up and shoot him, and one old man who had been with me on two or three occasions when I had followed up Isabeline and had thought me crazy for not having shot her instead of going miles and miles for the sake of 'looking' at her, was careful to inform me that it was not the mother with cubs that the villagers referred to.

It was June ere I got a chance of paying the dear old haunts a visit. Devil and Fool would now be twenty-eight months old and well able to look after themselves. Would I still be able to tell one from the other and when I did see them, would I forget all past associations and shoot on sight, or would I be as eager to watch their antics as of yore?

The second day after arriving on the scene, two bears were seen on a plateau some distance from camp, but too late in the evening to permit of my making a closer acquaintance on that day. Next morning I left camp before it was light and found myself far up on the highlands ere the first streaks of dawn touched the peaks ahead, and shortly after, my glasses revealed one solitary bear, and, if size was any criterion, the veteran who had done the damage among the flocks. Half an hour's careful talking brought me to within a few yards of where I had last seen him and a cautious look round showed him sitting on a patch of snow, meditating over his many misdeeds.

A low whistle roused him and he cocked his ears and peered round in the direction of the sound, but did not move his position. A depression in the ground served me admirably to run round and get in front of him, but he had heard me moving and was now on the alert though still sitting where I had left him. A snap shot was the work of a moment, and the monster's life blood dyed the white snow beneath him a bright crimson.

Later on I found Isabeline—alone. Devil and Fool had been driven from her side by the big beast whose hide now covers the floor, and the little mother roams the alpine pastures still, and has long forgotten the existence of her young hopefuls.

HUNTING WITH A CAMERA

F.W. Champion

On the left bank of the Ganges, a few miles below Lachmanjhula, in the United Provinces, where the holy river emerged from the Himalayan foothills, lies a great forest which forms the home of many wild beasts from the mighty elephant and tiger downwards. Haridwar, that sacred and populous Hindu city, is only a few miles away on the other side of the river, and the pious pilgrims who come from all over India to wash away their sins by bathing in the holy water little realize how often at night tigers stand on the opposite bank of the river to watch with curious gaze the bright illuminations of their festivals, or how these huge beasts even listen to the rumbling of the trains as they bring the pilgrims to the railway station after long journeys from all parts of India.

In this forest for many years has resided a very fine tigress, who has so far escaped destruction at the hands of the numerous sportsmen who are for ever pursuing her—and may she continue to do so until old age mars her pleasure in the life which is as dear to her as their own is to her hunters! She is very powerfully built for a tigress and is perhaps as fine an example of her race as is to be found anywhere in northern India. For this reason the hunter who at last lays her low will undoubtedly feel very pleased with himself, although there are some amongst us—an increasing number these days, one is glad to be able to say—who can derive just as much pleasure from hunting with the bloodless camera, which, after all, takes no life and is much less selfish than shooting to kill, in that the resultant pictures can subsequently give pleasure to others in a way that skins or horns can never do even though the skin be stolen from one of the finest tigresses in northern India.

I will now describe a few episodes which have occurred from time to time during the last four or five years when we happened to be camping within this tigress' domain and have thus had opportunities to hunt her with a camera. The first time we became acquainted with her was several years ago, when she suddenly took to killing the buffloes which the local bamboo-cutters use for dragging their produce down to the edge of the Ganges, where the bamboos are tied together into huge rafts and floated away to distant markets on the banks of the great Ganges canals—those fine monuments of the work of the Irrigation Department in Upper India. During a single week she killed four or five of these buffaloes and always left the carcases to be devoured by vultures after making one heavy meal. Several times, mounted on a tame elephant, we searched the places where we hoped she would be lying up during the day, but she was never there and it appeared that there were two reasons for this. Firstly, she had at the time two or three small cubs to feed, which meant that she had to kill more frequently than usual, whereas an attack of rinderpest had greatly reduced the numbers of the sambar which form her usual food; and, secondly, she had been fired at in a beat and missed, so that she had learnt not to lie near her kills in the daytime. The result was that several natural kills produced no single glimpse of her to enable us to take a photograph, although one day a fine chital stag with his horns in velvet allowed us to approach within a few yards and seemed little perturbed at the click of the shutter as we recorded his picture. His very presence there, however, was a fairly certain indication that the tigress was not where we were hoping to find her. On another occasion, having once more failed to find our quarry, we followed a poor specimen of a sambar stag for two or three hours in the hope that he would stand in a good light and give us an opportunity to take his photograph; but he always moved too quickly from one belt of thick shade to another and all we could do was to snap him standing half-hidden among some bushes. Oh! If only the animal-photographer could explain to wild animals that, were they to stand out in the open for a few moments in a good pose, he would take their photographs, give them an honoured place on his wall or in his collection of jungle pictures and let them depart in peace!

But we are wandering from the subject of our tigress and must return. As we have already seen, she never seemed to be near her kills in the daytime, and, as she generally left them in the open, they were usually devoured by jackals and vultures long before the evening. She soon gave up killing the dragging cattle, which was as well for her, because, although the loss of these cattle was largely due to the carelessness of their owners, who calmly left them loose at night in places which they knew the tigress might visit, I should otherwise have had to make an effort to destroy her in the interests of my forest employees. We then tried tying up young buffalo-baits in very quiet secluded spots; but we soon found that the only places where she would kill these baits were open cross-roads, which meant that hyenas and jackals—which frequent jungle roads—

always smelt them out and fired off the automatic flashlight arranged over the kills early in the evening and long before there was any hope of the tigress arriving. One day she killed a bait in a particularly quiet spot, and, full of hope, we mounted on a tame elephant and stalked the kill very quietly in the heat of the afternoon. Sure enough, we found her at last dozing in the shade of a bamboo clump and thus obtained our first view of her magnificent proportions. But she was evidently sleeping with one eye open, for, although there was ample time for a quick shot with a rifle, she dashed off with an angry 'whoof' just as I was getting her into focus on the mirror of my reflex camera, so that once more she got the better of us. This particular kill, however, did not fail altogether as one of her cubs, who was by now three-parts grown, returned during the night and was caught by our automatic flashlight in the act of seizing the kill.

The next stage in our efforts to secure her photograph involved sitting out all night over a live-bait tied near an old kill, which we hoped would attract her to the spot and perhaps induce her to attack the living bait, over which the flashlight apparatus had been arranged during the day time so that it could be fired by pulling a cord from the machan. The reader will now accompany me in thought to this machan and in imagination spend the night with me in the tree. We will assume that the difficult adjustments of the flashlight apparatus have already been done—they take several hours and we are now mounted on a tame elephant and approaching the chosen spot at about 4 p.m. on a fine warm afternoon. As we draw near the place, we move very slowly and approach carefully under cover, since tigers in general and this tigress in particular have a habit of doing the unexpected and who knows but that we may now find her calmly eating her kill in broad daylight. But no: she is not here at the moment. A short distance from the old kill stands a dead tree on which are perched a number of vultures, evidently resting after their disgusting meal of putrid flesh, and above in the crystal clear sky, is circling a kite, also attracted by the prospect of food. We pause for a moment to watch the wonderful grace of the movements of his forked tail, which is a hundredfold more efficient than the rudder of any ship or aeroplane invented by man, and then we move on again, noting as we approach the stealthy retreat of a pair of jackals, who have been stealing a meal during the absence of the rightful owner of the kill. We now climb up to the machan and, sending the elephant back to camp, settle down to the prospect of the deep enjoyment of a moonlight night spent absolutely alone in the heart of a great forest. All around us is a vast jungle containing no human being for miles in any direction, yet positively alive with wild animals and birds of every kind and description. Only a day or two previously a herd of about twenty wild elephants, including two or three tiny babies, passed under the very tree in which we are now sitting, and the place is notorious for sloth bears, which come from long distances to feed on the luscious crop of berries now ripening on the ber bushes all around us. The local sambar have been sadly thinned out by a recent attack of rinderpest, but chital are common in the neighbourhood, which, among many other species, even holds a few of those curious four-horned antelope nowhere common in the Himalayan foothills. And the birds! Who can give any idea of the marvellous beauty and variety of the feathered denizens of the foot-hill forests? All around us are scores of peafowl, attracted like the bears by the ripening of the jungle fruits; green paroquets in hundreds are dashing about at a tremendous pace in every direction and screaming with joy in harsh raucous tones as through they are revelling in the thrill of their rapid motion through the air; bulbuls are twittering on almost every bush; plover of two or three species are running about the dry sandy rau bed in front of us; two or three kites are screaming in the air above us; a pair of fantailed flycatchers are pirouetting from twig to twig of the very tree in which we are sitting; and a host of others of every conceivable shape and colours are to be seen and heard in the directions. All seem bubbling over with a happiness which finds ready expression in song and play. And yet some naturalists claim that all Nature is intensely cruel! Those of us, however, who enjoy watching rather than destroying wild creatures do not find Nature cruel—far from it. Sudden death appears at intervals, it is true, but it is only our vivid imagination and fear of the hereafter that make us afraid of death. Wild creatures do not know what death is and are not troubled by thoughts about Heaven and Hell, so that the sudden passing of one of their number as the result of the advent of some flesh-eating animal or bird is but a fleeting incident soon forgotten by the survivors. But once again we are straying from our subject.

We sit happily on in our machan, hoping against hope that at last the tigress will give us our chance to take her photograph and imperceptibly the day passes away to be replaced by the full glory of a jungle night. Once or twice we hear the alarm cry of a kakar or chital in the distance and hope surges up in our hearts, only to die down again as the cries soon cease. Then a curious rumbling comes from the direction of Haridwar, some distance away, and we wonder what tamasha there can be making such a disturbance. But the noise seems to be increasing, and, at last, straining over the edge of the machan, we realize with dismay that a heavy storm is rapidly approaching from the west. What are we to do? We have no mackintosh and little bedding and our camp is several miles away, with a jungle full of wild beasts in between and no lamp or path to help us get there. Yet if we stay in the machan we are bound to get wet through and thoroughly chilled, which will inevitably result in a bout of fever. Even as we consider the problem the moon disappears, dazzling lightning flashes across the sky in all directions, a strong wind begins to blow, and down comes a tropical deluge of rain which soon soaks the camera, flashlight, blankets, and finally us. All hope of our long-sought picture has gone, and, feeling distinctly nervous of being struck by lighting, we see in imagination our tigress hugging herself with glee at the thought of how well we are being punished for having had the impertinence to continue for so long in the vain pursuit of her photograph. At long last, after we have become resigned to spending a night of misery, we hear a curious whistling which does not seem to come from any animal or bird we recognize. Surely we are not beginning to get a little light in the head as a result of our nerve-racking experience? No: the whistling continues and increases in volume so that at last we realize, with a thrill of joy, that it must be one of our tame elephants, which, despite our orders to the contrary, has been sent out by my wife to rescue us from our predicament. We eagerly call up the elephant, thankful to escape from our chilly damp perch, and rapidly return to our comfortable camp four miles away, which we reach about 1 a.m. Shortly afterwards, fortified by hot Bovril, we are dozing in a comfortable warm bed and dreaming of new schemes for obtaining the photograph which had now become a fetish with us.

Thus the campaign continued for some years, but always without success. We could never find her again by stalking in the daytime; she always seemed to discover our presence if we sat in machans over her kills at night; and, if we arranged our automatic flashlight apparatus over her kills, she waited until hyenas and jackals had spent some time there first and thus fired the flashlight before she was due to appear. It seemed as though she were going to win in this contest of wits, and then, at last, we had a brilliant idea. We had a kill one day on the edge of a broad rau bed and we had noticed previously, from a study of her tracks, that she had formed the habit of hugging the foot of a low bank on the edge of this rau bed when passing this particular locality. How would it be if we were to arrange a tripwire at the edge of this bank, some distance from the kill, and thus avoid the risk of the chance being ruined by the inevitable jackals and hyenas? There seemed some hope of this method proving successful, especially as we had a good idea of the direction from which she was likely to arrive and could thus probably guide her, all unconsciously, by means of a judicious arrangement of cut branches, to the exact spot where our photographic trap was to be set. We decided to carry out this plan and arranged our apparatus with extreme care, even to the last detail of a trip-wire carefully matched to the colour of the surrounding ground for she had seen one of our trip-wires once before and carefully stepped over it without touching it! We then returned to our camp with a sneaking hope that at long last we stood a fair chance of winning in the long-drawn-out battle of wits. About midnight we heard the familiar boom of the exploding flashlight and we were so excited that we jumped out of bed and hurried out to the spot by the light of a lantern. Had we really succeeded at last, or had those...hyenas and jackals once more ruined a good chance? After what seemed a tremendous time, although in reality the distance was quite short, we at last reached the spot and—hurrah! There were the tell-tale claw marks in the gound as she had involuntarily extended her claws on being startled by the noise and light of the exploding flashlight. Yes: the complicated mechanism of tripping the shutter had also worked without a hitch—it does not always do so—and at last our plate had been exposed. Now for the final stage of development. We rushed back to our camp, and, although it was the middle of the night, out came the developing chemicals, and before many minutes had passed we had the tremendous satisfaction of seeing a fine negative appearing in the developing dish—a negative which, except for a slight fault in one of the fore-legs, is as good as we had ever hoped to obtain even in our most optimistic moments.

Thus ended the hunt for the first negative of this fine tigress, to whom we take off our hats with heartfelt thanks for having given us such a fine run for our money. We could have shot her years before when we first saw her, and, had we done so, all would have been over except for a skin which would have begun rotting away by now under the effects of this trying climate. Yet she lives on and may still provide us with more harmless pleasure, so who can now say that, once we have overcome our primitive and savage lust of killing, hunting with a camera is not the peer of any form of blood-hunting that the world can produce.

THE BEAST WITH FIVE FINGERS

W.F. Harvey

The story, I suppose, begins with Adrian Borlsover, whom I met when I was a little boy and he an old man. My father had called to appeal for a subscription, and before he left, Mr Borlsover laid his right hand in blessing on my head. I shall never forget the awe in which I gazed up at his face and realized for the first time that eyes might be dark and beautiful and shining, and yet not able to see.

For Adrian Borlsover was blind.

He was an extraordinary man, who came of an eccentric stock. Borlsover sons for some reason always seemed to marry very ordinary women, which perhaps accounted for the fact that no Borlsover had been a genius, and only one Borlsover had been mad. But they were great champions of little causes, generous patrons of odd sciences, founders of querulous sects, trustworthy guides to the bypath meadows of erudition.

Adrian was an authority on the fertilization of orchids. He had held at one time the family living at Borlsover Conyers, until a congenital weakness of the lungs obliged him to seek a less rigorous climate in the sunny south-coast watering-place where I had seen him. Occasionally, he would relieve one or other of the local clergy. My father described him as a fine preacher, who gave long and inspiring sermons from what many men would have considered unprofitable texts. 'An excellent proof,' he would add, 'of the truth of the doctrine of direct verbal inspiration.'

Adrian Borlsover was exceedingly clever with his hands. His penmanship was exquisite. He illustrated all his scientific papers, made his own woodcuts, and carved the reredos that is at present the chief feature of interest in the church at Borlsover Conyers. He had an exceedingly clever knack in cutting silhouettes for young ladies and paper pigs and cows for little children, and made more than one complicated wind instrument of his own devising.

When he was fifty years old, Adrian Borlsover lost his sight. In a wonderfully short time he adapted himself to the new conditions of life. He quickly learnt to read Braille. So marvellous indeed was his sense of touch, that he was still able to maintain his interest in botany. The mere passing of his long supple fingers over a flower was sufficient means for its identification, though occasionally he would use his lips. I have found several letters of his among my father's correspondence; in no case was there anything to show that he was afflicted with blindness, and this in spite of the fact that he exercised undue economy in the spacing of lines. Towards the close of his life, Adrian Borlsover was credited with the powers of touch that seemed almost uncanny. It has been said that he could tell at once the colour of a ribbon placed between his fingers. My father would neither confirm nor deny the story.

Adrian Borlsover was a bachelor. His elder brother, Charles, had married late in life, leaving one son, Eustace, who lived in the gloomy Georgian mansion at Borlsover Conyers, where he could work undisturbed in collecting material for his great book on heredity.

Like his uncle, he was a remarkable man. The Borlsovers had always been born naturalists, but Eustace possessed in a special degree the power of systematizing his knowledge. He had received his university education in Germany; and then, after post-graduate work in Vienna and Naples, had travelled for four years in South America and the East, getting together a huge store of material for a new study into the processes of variation.

He lived alone at Borlsover Conyers with Saunders, his secretary, a man who bore a somewhat dubious reputation in the district, but whose powers as a mathematician, combined with his business abilities, were invaluable to Eustace.

Uncle and nephew saw little of each other. The visits of Eustace were confined to a week in the summer or autumn— tedious weeks, that dragged almost as slowly as the bath-chair in which the old man was drawn along the sunny sea-front. In their way the two men were fond of each other, though their intimacy would, doubtless, have been greater, had they shared the same religious views. Adrian held to the old-fashioned evangelical dogmas of his early manhood; his nephew for many years had been thinking of embracing Buddhism. Both men possessed, too, the reticence the Borlsovers had always shown, and which their enemies sometimes called hypocrisy. With Adrian it was a reticence as to the things he had left undone; but with Eustace it seemed that the curtain which he was so careful to leave undrawn hid something more than a half-empty chamber.

Two years before his death, Adrian Borlsover developed, unknown to himself, the not uncommon power of automatic writing. Eustace made the discovery by accident. Adrian was sitting reading in bed, the forefinger of his left hand tracing the Braille characters, when his nephew noticed that a pencil the old man held in his right hand was moving slowly along the opposite page. He left his seat in the window and sat down beside the bed. The right hand continued to move, and now he could see plainly that they were letters and words which it was forming.

'Adrian Borlsover,' wrote the hand, 'Eustace Borlsover, Charles Borlsover, Francis Borlsover, Sigismund Borlsover, Adrian Borlsover, Eustace Borlsover, Saville Borlsover. B for Borlsover. Honesty is the Best Policy. Beautiful Belinda Borlsover.'

'What curious nonsense!' said Eustace to himself.

'King George ascended the throne in 1760,' wrote the hand. 'Crowd, a noun of multitude; a collection of individuals. Adrian Borlsover, Eustace Borlsover.'

'It seems to me,' said his uncle, closing the book, 'that you had much better make the most of the afternoon sunshine and take your walk now.'

'I think perhaps I will,' Eustace answered as he picked up the volume. 'I won't go far, and when I come back, I can read to you those articles in *Nature* about which we were speaking.'

He went along the promenade, but stopped at the first shelter, and, seating himself in the corner best protected from the wind, he examined the book at leisure. Nearly every page was scored with a meaningless jumble of pencil-marks; rows of capital letters, short words, long words, complete sentences, copy-book tags. The whole thing, in fact had the appearance of a copy-book, and, on a more careful scrutiny, Eustace thought that there was ample evidence to show that the handwriting at the beginning of the book, good though it was, was not nearly so good as the handwriting at the end.

He left his uncle at the end of October with a promise to return early in December. It seemed to him quite clear that the old man's power of automatic writing was developing rapidly, and for the first time he looked forward to a visit that would combine duty with interest.

But on his return he was at first disappointed. His uncle, he thought, looked older. He was listless, too, preferring others to read to him and dictating nearly all his letters. Not until the day before he left had Eustace an opportunity of observing Adrian Borlsover's new-found faculty.

The old man, propped up in bed with pillows, had sunk into a light sleep. His two hands lay on the coverlet, his left hand tightly clasping his right. Eustace took an empty manuscript-book and placed a pencil within reach of the fingers of the right hand. They snatched at it eagerly, then dropped the pencil to loose the left hand from its restraining grasp.

'Perhaps to prevent interference I had better hold that hand,' said Eustace to himself, as he watched the pencil. Almost immediately it began to write.

'Blundering Borlsovers, unnecessarily unnatural, extraordinarily eccentric, culpably curious.'

'Who are you?' asked Eustace in a low voice.

'Never you mind,' wrote the hand of Adrian.

'Is it my uncle who is writing?'

'O my prophetic soul, mine uncle!'

'Is it anyone I know?'

'Silly Eustace, you'll see me very soon.'

'When shall I see you?'

'When poor old Adrian's dead.'

'Where shall I see you?'

'Where shall you not?'

Instead of speaking his next question, Eustace wrote it. 'What is the time?'

The fingers dropped the pencil and moved three or four times across the paper. Then, picking up the pencil, they wrote: 'Ten minutes before four. Put your book away, Eustace. Adrian mustn't find us working at this sort of thing. He doesn't know what to make of it, and I won't have poor old Adrian disturbed. Au revoir!'

Adrian Borlsover awoke with a start.

'I've been dreaming again,' he said; 'such queer dreams of leaguered cities and forgotten towns. You were mixed up in this one, Eustace, though I can't remember how. Eustace, I want to warn you. Don't walk in doubtful paths. Choose your friends well. Your poor grandfather...'

A fit of coughing put an end to what he was saying, but Eustace saw that the hand was still writing. He managed unnoticed to draw the book away. 'I'll light the gas,' he said, 'and ring for tea.' On the other side of the bed-curtain he saw the last sentences that had been written.

'It's too late, Adrian,' he read. 'We're friends already, aren't we, Eustace Borlsover?'

On the following day Eustace left. He thought his uncle looked ill when he said goodbye, and the old man spoke despondently of the failure his life had been.

'Nonsense, uncle,' said his nephew. 'You have got over your difficulties in a way not one in a hundred thousand would have done. Everyone marvels at your splendid perseverance in teaching your hand to take the place of your lost sight. To me it's been a revelation of the possibilities of education.'

'Education,' said his uncle dreamily, as if the word had started a new train of thought. 'Education is good so long as you know to whom and for what purpose you give it. But with the lower orders of men, the base and more sordid spirits, I have grave doubts as to its results. Well, goodbye, Eustace; I may not see you again. You are a true Borlsover, with all the Borlsover faults. Marry, Eustace. Marry some good, sensible girl. And if by any chance I don't see you again, my will is at my solicitor's. I've not left you any legacy, because I know you're well-provided for; but I thought you might like to have my books. Oh, and there's just one other thing. You know, before the end people often lose control over themselves and make absurd requests. Don't pay any attention to them, Eustace. Goodbye!' and he held out his hand. Eustace took it. It remained in his a fraction of a second longer than he had expected and gripped him with a virility that was surprising. There was, too, in its touch a subtle sense of intimacy.

'Why, uncle,' he said, 'I shall see you alive and well for many long years to come.'

Two months later Adrian Borlsover died.

Eustace Borlsover was in Naples at the time. He read the obituary notice in the *Morning Post* on the day announced for the funeral.

'Poor old fellow!' he said. 'I wonder whether I shall find room for all his books.'

The question occurred to him again with greater force when three days later, he found himself standing in the library at Borlsover Conyers, a huge room built for use and not for beauty in the year of Waterloo by a Borlsover who was an ardent admirer of the great Napoleon. It was arranged on the plan of many college libraries, with tall projecting bookcases forming deep recesses of dusty silence, fit graves for the old hates of forgotten controversy, the dead passions of forgotten lives. At the end of the room, behind the bust of some unknown eighteenth-century divine, an ugly iron corkscrew stair led to a shelf-lined gallery. Nearly, every shelf was full.

'I must talk to Saunders about it,' said Eustace. 'I suppose that we shall have to have the billiard-room fitted up with bookcases.'

The two men met for the first time after many weeks in the dining-room that evening.

'Hallo!' said Eustace, standing before the fire with his hands in his pockets. 'How goes the world, Saunders? Why these dress togs?' He himself was wearing an old shooting-jacket. He did not believe in mourning, as he had told his uncle on his last visit; and, though he usually went in for quiet-coloured ties, he wore this evening one of an ugly red, in order to shock Morton, the butler, and to make them thrash out the whole question of mourning for themselves in the servants' hall. Eustace was a true Borlsover. 'The world,' said Saunders, 'goes the same as usual, confoundedly slow. The dress togs are accounted for by an invitation from Captain Lockwood to bridge.'

'How are you getting there?'

'There's something the matter with the car, so I've told Jackson to drive me round in the dogcart. Any objection?'

'O dear me, no! We've had all things in common for far too many years for me to raise objections at this hour of the day.'

'You'll find your correspondence in the library,' went on Saunders. 'Most of it I've seen to. There are a few private letters I haven't opened. There's also a box with a rat or something inside it that came by the evening post. Very likely it's the six-toed beast Terry was sending us to cross with the four-toed albino. I didn't look because I didn't want to mess up my things; but I should gather from the way it's jumping about that it's pretty hungry'

'Oh, I'll see to it,' said Eustace, 'while you and the captain earn an honest penny.'

Dinner over and Saunders gone, Eustace went into the library. Though the fire had been lit, the room was by no means cheerful.

'We'll have all the lights on, at any rate,' he said, as he turned the switches. 'And, Morton,' he added, when the butler brought the coffee, 'get me a screwdriver or something to undo this box. Whatever the animal is, he's kicking up the deuce of a row. What is it? Why are you dawdling?'

'If you please, sir, when the postman brought it, he told me that they'd bored the holes in the lid at the post office. There were no breathing holes in the lid, sir, and they didn't want the animal to die. That is all, sir.'

'It's culpably careless of the man, whoever he was,' said Eustace as he removed the screws, 'packing an animal like this in a wooden box with no means of getting air. Confound it all! I meant to ask Morton to bring me a cage to put it in. Now I suppose I shall have to get one myself.'

He placed a heavy book on the lid from which the screws had been removed, and went into the billiard-room. As he came back into the library with an empty cage in his hand, he heard the sound of something falling, and then of something scuttling along the floor.

'Bother it! The beast's got out. How in the world am I to find it again in this library?'

To search for it did indeed seem hopeless. He tried to follow the sound of the scuttling in one of the recesses, where the animal seemed to be running behind the books on the shelves; but it was impossible to locate it. Eustace resolved to go on quietly reading. Very likely the animal might gain confidence and show itself Saunders seemed to have dealt in his usual methodical manner with most of the correspondence. There were still the private letters.

What was that? Two sharp clicks and the lights in the hideous candelabra that hung from the ceiling suddenly went out.

'I wonder if something has gone wrong with the fuse,' said Eustace, as he went to the switches by the door. Then he stopped. There was a noise at the other end of the room, as if something was crawling up the iron corkscrew stair. 'If it's gone into the gallery,' he said, 'well and good.' He hastily turned on the lights, crossed the room, and climbed up the stair. But he could see nothing. His grandfather had placed a little gate at the top of the stair, so that children could run and romp in the gallery without fear of accident. This Eustace closed, and, having considerably narrowed the circle of his search, returned to his desk by the fire.

How gloomy the library was! There was no sense of intimacy about the room. The few busts that an eighteenth-century Borlsover had brought back from the grand tour might have been in keeping in the old library. Here they seemed out of place. They made the room feel cold in spite of the heavy red damask curtains and great gilt cornices.

With a crash two heavy books fell from the gallery to the floor; then, as Borlsover looked, another, and yet another.

'Very well. You'll starve for this, my beauty!' he said. 'We'll do some little experiments on the metabolism of rats deprived of water. Go on! Chuck them down! I think I've got the upper hand.' He turned once more to his correspondence. The letter was from the family solicitor. It spoke of his uncle's death, and of the valuable collection of books that had been left to him in the will.

'There was one request [he read] which certainly came as

a surprise to me. As you know, Mr Adrian Borlsover had left instructions that his body was to be buried in as simple a manner as possible at Eastbourne. He expressed a desire that there should be neither wreaths nor flowers of any kind, and hoped that his friends and relatives would not consider it necessary to wear mourning. The day before his death we received a letter cancelling these instructions. He wished the body to be embalmed (he gave us the address of the man we were to employ—Pennifer, Ludgate Hill), with orders that his right hand should be sent to you stating that it was at your special request. The other arrangements about the funeral remained unaltered.'

'Good Lord,' said Eustace, 'what in the world was the old boy driving at? And what in the name of all that's holy is that?'

Someone was in the gallery. Someone had pulled the cord attached to one of the blinds, and it had rolled up with a snap. Someone must be in the gallery, for a second blind did the same. Someone must be walking round the gallery, for one after the other the blinds sprang up, letting in the moonlight.

'I haven't got to the bottom of this yet,' said Eustace, 'but I will do, before the night is very much older'; and he hurried up the corkscrew stair. He had just got to the top when the lights went out a second time, and he heard again the scuttling along the floor. Quickly he stole on tiptoe in the dim moonshine in the direction of the noise, feeling, as he went, for one of the switches. His fingers touched the metal knob at last. He turned on the electric light.

About ten yards in front of him, crawling along the floor, was a man's hand. Eustace stared at it in utter amazement. It was moving quickly in the manner of a geometer caterpillar, the fingers humped up one moment, flattened out the next; the thumb appeared to give a crablike motion all the while. While he was looking, too surprised to stir, the hand disappeared round the corner. Eustace ran forward. He no longer saw it, but he could hear it, as it squeezed its way behind the books on one of the shelves. A heavy volume had been displaced. There was a gap in the row of books, where it had got in. In his fear lest it should escape him again, he seized the first book that came to his hand and plugged it into the hole. Then, emptying two shelves of their contents, he took the wooden boards and propped them up in front to make his barrier doubly sure.

'I wish Saunders was back,' he said; 'one can't tackle this sort of thing alone.' It was after eleven, and there seemed little likelihood of Saunders returning before twelve. He did not dare to leave the shelf unwatched, even to run downstairs to ring the bell. Morton, the butler, often used to come round about eleven to see that the windows were fastened, but he might not come. Eustace was thoroughly unstrung. At last he heard steps down below.

'Morton!' he shouted. 'Morton!'

'Sir?'

'Has Mr Saunders got back yet?'

'Not yet, sir.'

'Well, bring me some brandy, and hurry up about it. I'm up in the gallery, you duffer.'

'Thanks,' said Eustace, as he emptied the glass. 'Don't go to bed yet, Morton. There are a lot of books that have fallen down by accident. Bring them up and put them back on their shelves.'

Morton had never seen Borlsover in so talkative a mood as on that night. 'Here,' said Eustace, when the books had been put back and dusted, 'you might hold up these boards for me, Morton. That beast in the box got out, and I've been chasing it all over the place.'

'I think I can hear it chewing at the books, sir. They're not valuable, I hope? I think that's the carriage, sir; I'll go and call Mr Saunders.'

It seemed to Eustace that he was away for five minutes, but it could hardly have been more than one, when he returned with Saunders. 'All right, Morton, you can go now. I'm up here, Saunders.'

'What's all the row?' asked Saunders, as he lounged forward with his hands in his pockets. The luck had been with him all the evening. He was completely satisfied, both with himself and with Captain Lockwood's taste in wines. 'What's the matter? You look to me to be in an absolutely blue funk.'

'That old devil of an uncle of mine,' began Eustace—'Oh, I can't explain it all. It's his hand that's been playing Old Harry all the evening. But I've got it cornered behind these books. You've got to help me to catch it.'

'What's up with you, Eustace? What's the game?'

'It's no game, you silly idiot! If you don't believe me, take out one of those books and put your hand in and feel.'

'All right,' said Saunders; 'but wait till I've rolled up my sleeve. The accumulated dust of centuries, eh?' He took off his coat, knelt down, and thrust his arm along the shelf.

'There's something there right enough,' he said. 'It's got a funny, stumpy end to it, whatever it is, and nips like a crab. Ah! no, you don't!' He pulled his hand out in a flash. 'Shove in a book quickly. Now it can't get out.'

'What was it?' asked Eustace.

'Something that wanted very much to get hold of me. I felt what seemed like a thumb and forefinger. Give me some brandy.'

'How are we to get it out of there?'

'What about a landing-net?'

'No good. It would be too smart for us. I tell you, Saunders, it can cover the ground far faster than I can walk. But I think I see how we can manage it. The two books at the end of the shelf are big ones, that go right back against the wall. The others are very thin. I'll take out one at a time, and you slide the rest along, until we have it squashed between the end two.'

It certainly seemed to be the best plan. One by one as they took out the books, the space behind grew smaller and smaller. There was something in it that was certainly very much alive. Once they caught sight of fingers feeling for a way of escape. At last they had it pressed between the two big books.

'There's muscle there, if there isn't warm flesh and blood,' said Saunders, as he held them together. 'It seems to be a hand right enough, too. I suppose this is a sort of infectious hallucination. I've read about such cases before.'

'Infectious fiddlesticks!' said Eustace, his face white with anger; 'bring the thing downstairs. We'll get it back into the box.'

It was not altogether easy, but they were successful at last. 'Drive in the screws,' said Eustace; 'we won't run any risks. Put the box in this old desk of mine. There's nothing in it that I want. Here's the key. Thank goodness there's nothing wrong with the lock.'

'Quite a lively evening,' said Saunders. 'Now let's hear more about your uncle.'

They sat up together until early morning. Saunders had no desire for sleep. Eustace was trying to explain and to forget; to conceal from himself a fear that he had never felt before—the fear of walking alone down the long corridor to his bedroom.

'Whatever it was,' said Eustace to Saunders on the following morning, 'I propose that we drop the subject. There's nothing to keep us here for the next ten days. We'll motor up to the Lakes and get some climbing.'

'And see nobody all day, and sit bored to death with each other every night. Not for me, thanks. Why not run up to town? Run's the exact word in this case, isn't it? We're both in such a blessed funk. Pull yourself together, Eustace, and let's have another look at the hand.'

'As you like,' said Eustace; 'there's the key.'

They went into the library and opened the desk. The box was as they had left it on the previous night.

'What are you waiting for?' asked Eustace.

'I am waiting for you to volunteer to open the lid. However since you seem to funk it, allow me. There doesn't seem to be the likelihood of any rumpus this morning at all events.' He opened the lid and picked out the hand.

'Cold?' asked Eustace.

'Tepid. A bit below blood heat by the feel. Soft and supple too. If it's the embalming, it's a sort of embalming I've never seen before. Is it your uncle's hand?'

'Oh yes, it's his all right,' said Eustace. 'I should know those long thin fingers anywhere. Put it back in the box, Saunders. Never mind about the screws. I'll lock the desk, so that there'll be no chance of its getting out. We'll compromise by motoring up to town for a week. If we can get off soon after lunch, we ought to be at Grantham or Stamford by night.'

'Right,' said Saunders, 'and tomorrow—oh, well, by tomorrow we shall have forgotten all about this beastly thing.'

If, when the morrow came, they had not forgotten, it was certainly true that at the end of the week they were able to tell a very vivid ghost-story at the little supper Eustace gave on Halloween.

'You don't want us to believe that it's true, Mr Borlsover? How perfectly awful!'

'I'll take my oath on it, and so would Saunders here; wouldn't you, old chap?'

'Any number of oaths,' said Saunders. 'It was a long thin hand, you know, and it gripped me just like that.'

'Don't, Mr Saunders! Don't! How perfectly horrid! Now tell us another one, do! Only a really creepy one, please.'

'Here's a pretty mess!' said Eustace on the following day, as he threw a letter across the table to Saunders. 'It's your affair, though. Mrs Merrit, if I understand it, gives a month's notice.'

'Oh, that's quite absurd on Mrs Merrit's part,' replied Saunders. 'She doesn't know what she's talking about. Let's see what she says.'

> Dear Sir [he read]. This is to let you know that I must give you a month's notice as from Tuesday, the 13th. For a long time I've felt the place too big for me; but when Jane Parfit and Emma Laidlaw go off with scarcely as much as an "If you please", after frightening the wits out of the other girls, so that they can't turn out a room by themselves or walk alone down the stairs for fear of treading on half-frozen toads or hearing it run along the passages at night, all I can say is that it's no place for me. So I must ask you, Mr Borlsover, sir, to find a new housekeeper, that has no objection to large and lonely houses, which some people do say, not that I believe them for a minute, my poor mother always having been a Wesleyan, are haunted.
>
> Yours faithfully,
>
> Elizabeth Merrit.
>
> PS.—I should be obliged if you would give my respects

to Mr Saunders. I hope that he won't run any risks with his cold.

'Saunders,' said Eustace, 'you've always had a wonderful way with you in dealing with servants. You mustn't let poor old Merrit go.'

'Of course she shan't go,' said Saunders. 'She's probably only angling for a rise in salary. I'll write to her this morning.'

'No. There's nothing like a personal interview. We've had enough of town. We'll go back tomorrow, and you must work your cold for all it's worth. Don't forget that it's got on to the chest, and will require weeks of feeding up and nursing.'

'All right; I think I can manage Mrs Merrit.'

But Mrs Merrit was more obstinate than he had thought. She was very sorry to hear of Mr Saunders's cold, and how he lay awake all night in London coughing; very sorry indeed. She'd change his room for him, gladly, and get the south room aired, and wouldn't he have a hot basin of bread and milk last thing at night? But she was afraid that she would have to leave at the end of the month.

'Try her with an increase of salary,' was the advice of Eustace.

It was no use. Mrs Merrit was obdurate, though she knew of a Mrs Goddard, who had been housekeeper to Lord Gargrave, who might be glad to come at the salary mentioned.

'What's the matter with the servants, Morton?' asked Eustace that evening, when he brought the coffee into the library. 'What's all this about Mrs Merrit wanting to leave?'

'If you please, sir, I was going to mention it myself. I have a confession to make, sir. When I found your note, asking me to open that desk and take out the box with the rat, I broke the lock, as you told me, and was glad to do it, because I could hear the animal in the box making a great noise, and I thought it wanted food. So I took out the box, sir, and got a cage, and was going to transfer it, when the animal got away.'

'What in the world are you talking about? I never wrote any such note.'

'Excuse me, sir; it was the note I picked up here on the floor on the day you and Mr Saunders left. I have it in my pocket now.'

It certainly seemed to be in Eustace's handwriting. It was written in pencil, and began somewhat abruptly.

'Get a hammer, Morton,' he read, 'or some other tool and break open the lock in the old desk in the library. Take out the box that is inside. You need not do anything else. The lid is already open. Eustace Borlsover.'

'And you opened the desk?'

'Yes, sir; and, as I was getting the cage ready, the animal hopped out.'

'What animal?'

'The animal inside the box, sir.'

'What did it look like?'

'Well, sir, I couldn't tell you,' said Morton nervously. 'My back was turned, and it was halfway down the room when I looked up.'

'What was its colour?' asked Saunders. 'Black?'

'Oh no, sir; a greyish white. It crept along in a very funny way, sir. I don't think it had a tail.'

'What did you do then?'

'I tried to catch it; but it was no use. So I set the rat-traps and kept the library shut. Then that girl, Emma Laidlaw, left the door open when she was cleaning, and I think it must have escaped.'

'And you think it is the animal that's been frightening the maids?'

'Well, no sir, not quite. They said it was—you'll excuse me sir—a hand that they saw. Emma trod on it once at the bottom of the stairs. She thought then it was a half-frozen toad, only white. And then Parfit was washing up the dishes in the scullery. She wasn't thinking about anything in particular. It was close on dusk. She took her hands out of the water and was drying them absent-minded like on the roller towel, when she found she was drying someone else's hand as well, only colder than hers.'

'What nonsense!' exclaimed Saunders.

'Exactly sir; that's what I told her; but we couldn't get her to stop.'

'You don't believe all this?' said Eustace, turning suddenly towards the butler.

'Me, sir? Oh no, sir! I've not seen anything.'

'Nor heard anything?'

'Well, sir, if you must know, the bells do ring at odd times, and there's nobody there when we go; and when we go round to draw the blinds of a night, as often as not somebody's been there before us. But, as I says to Mrs Merrit, a young monkey might do wonderful things, and we all know that Mr Borlsover has had some strange animals about the place.'

'Very well, Morton, that will do.'

'What do you make of it?' asked Saunders, when they were alone. 'I mean of the letter he said you wrote.'

'Oh, that's simple enough,' said Eustace. 'See the paper it's written on? I stopped using that paper years ago, but there were a few odd sheets and envelopes left in the old desk. We never fastened up the lid of the box before locking it in. The hand got out, found a pencil, wrote this note, and shoved it through the crack on to the floor, where Morton found it. That's plain as daylight.'

'But the hand couldn't write!'

'Couldn't it? You've not seen it do the things I've seen.'

And he told Saunders more of what had happened at Eastbourne.

'Well,' said Saunders, 'in that case we have at least an explanation of the legacy. It was the hand which wrote, unknown to your uncle, that letter to your solicitor bequeathing itself to you. Your uncle had no more to do with that request than I. In fact, it would seem that he had some idea of this automatic writing and feared it.'

'Then if it's not my uncle, what is it?'

'I suppose some people might say that a disembodied spirit had got your uncle to educate and prepare a little body for it. Now it's got into that little body and is off on its own.'

'Well, what are we to do?'

'We'll keep our eyes open,' said Saunders, 'and try to catch it. If we can't do that, we shall have to wait till the bally clockwork runs down. After all, if it's flesh and blood, it can't live forever.'

For two days nothing happened. Then Saunders saw it sliding down the banister in the hall. He was taken unawares and lost a full second before he started in pursuit, only to find that the thing had escaped him. Three days later Eustace, writing alone in the library at night, saw it sitting on an open book at the other end of the room. The fingers crept over the page, as if it were reading; but before he had time to get up from his seat, it had taken the alarm, and was pulling itself up the curtains. Eustace watched it grimly, as it hung on to the cornice with three fingers and flicked thumb and forefinger at him in an expression of scornful derisio.

'I know what I'll do,' he said. 'If I only get it into the open I'll set the dogs on to it.'

He spoke to Saunders of the suggestion.

'It's a jolly good idea,' he said; 'only we won't wait till we find it out of doors. We'll get the dogs. There are the two terriers and the under-keeper's Irish mongrel, that's on to rats like a flash. Yom-spaniel has not got spirit enough for this sort of game.'

They brought the dogs into the house, and the keeper's Irish mongrel chewed up the slippers, and the terriers tripped up Morton as he waited at table; but all three were welcome. Even false security is better than no security at all.

For a fortnight nothing happened. Then the hand was caught not by the dogs, but by Mrs Merrit's grey parrot. The bird was in the habit of periodically removing the pins that kept its seed- and water-tin in place, and of escaping through the holes in the side of the cage. When once at liberty, Peter would show no inclination to return, and would often be about the house for days. Now, after six consecutive weeks of captivity, Peter had again discovered a new way of unloosing his bolts and was, at large, exploring the tapestried forests of the curtains and singing songs in praise of liberty from cornice and picture rail.

'It's no use your trying to catch him,' said Eustace to Mrs Merrit, as she came into the study one afternoon towards dusk with a step-ladder. 'You'd much better leave Peter alone. Starve him into surrender, Mrs Merrit; and don't leave bananas and seed about for him to peck at when he fancies he's hungry. You're far too soft-hearted.'

'Well, sir, I see he's right out of reach now on that picture-rail; so if you wouldn't mind closing the door, sir, when you leave the room, I'll bring his cage in tonight and put some meat inside it. He's that fond of meat, though it does make him pull out his feathers to suck the quills. They *do* say that if you cook—'

'Never mind, Mrs Merrit,' said Eustace, who was busy writing; 'that will do; I'll keep an eye on the bird.'

For a short time there was silence in the room.

'Scratch poor Peter,' said the bird. 'Scratch poor old Peter!'

'Be quiet, you beastly bird!'

'Poor old Peter! Scratch poor Peter; do!'

'I'm more likely to wring your neck, if I get hold of you.' He looked up at the picture-rail, and there was the hand, holding on to a hook with three fingers, and slowly scratching the head of the parrot with the fourth. Eustace ran to the bell and pressed it hard; then across to the window, which he closed with a bang. Frightened by the noise, the parrot shook its wings preparatory to flight, and, as it did so, the fingers of the hand got hold of it by the throat. There was a shrill scream from Peter, as he fluttered across the room, wheeling round in circles that ever descended, borne down under the weight that clung to him. The bird dropped at last quite suddenly, and Eustace saw fingers and feathers rolled into an inextricable mass on the floor. The struggle abruptly ceased, as finger and thumb squeezed the neck; the bird's eyes rolled up to show the white, and there was a faint, half-choked gurgle. But, before the fingers had time to loose their hold, Eustace had them in his own.

'Send Mr Saunders here at once,' he said to the maid who came in answer to the bell. 'Tell him I want him immediately.'

Then he went with the hand to the fire. There was a ragged gash across the back, where the bird's beak had torn it, but no blood oozed from the wound. He noted with disgust that the nails had grown long and discoloured.

'I'll burn the beastly thing,' he said. But he could not burn it He tried to throw it into the flames, but his own hands, as if impelled by some old primitive feeling, would not let him.

And so Saunders found him, pale and irresolute, with the hand still clasped tightly in his fingers.

'I've got it at last,' he said, in a tone of triumph.

'Good, let's have a look at it.'

'Not when it's loose. Get me some nails and a hammer and a board of some sort.'

'Can you hold it all right?'

'Yes, the thing's quite limp; tired out with throttling poor old Peter, I should say.'

'And now,' said Saunders, when he returned with the things, 'what are we going to do?'

'Drive a nail through it first, so that it can't get away. Then we can take our time over examining it.'

'Do it yourself,' said Saunders. 'I don't mind helping you with guinea-pigs occasionally, when there's something to be learned, partly because I don't fear a guinea-pig's revenge. This thing's different.'

'Oh, my aunt!' he giggled hysterically, 'look at it now.' For the hand was writhing in agonized contortions, squirming and wriggling upon the nail like a worm upon the hook.

'Well,' said Saunders, 'you've done it now. I'll leave you to examine it.'

'Don't go, in heaven's name! Cover it up, man; cover it up! Shove a cloth over it! Here!' and he pulled off the antimacassar from the back of a chair and wrapped the board in it. 'Now get the keys from my pocket and open the safe. Chuck the other things out. Oh, Lord, it's getting itself into frightful knots! Open it quick!' He threw the thing in and banged the door.

'We'll keep it there till it dies,' he said. 'May I burn in hell, if I ever open the door of that safe again.'

Mrs Merrit departed at the end of the month. Her

successor, Mrs Handyside, certainly was more successful in the management of the servants. Early in her rule she declared that she would stand no nonsense, and gossip soon withered and died.

'I shouldn't be surprised if Eustace married one of these days,' said Saunders. 'Well, I'm in no hurry for such an event. I know him far too well for the future Mrs Borlsover to like me. It will be the same old story again; a long friendship slowly made—marriage—and a long friendship quickly forgotten.'

But Eustace did not follow the advice of his uncle and marry. Old habits crept over and covered his new experience. He was, if anything, less morose, and showed a great inclination to take his natural part in country society.

Then came the burglary. The man, it was said, broke into the house by way of the conservatory. It was really little more than an attempt, for they only succeeded in carrying away a few pieces of plate from the pantry. The safe in the study was certainly found open and empty, but, as Mr Borlsover informed the police inspector, he had kept nothing of value in it during the last six months.

'Then you're lucky in getting off so easily, sir,' the man replied. 'By the way they have gone about their business I should say the were experienced cracksmen. They must have caught the alarm when they were just beginning their evening's work.'

'Yes,' said Eustace, 'I suppose I am lucky.'

'I've no doubt,' said the inspector, 'that we shall be able to trace the men. I've said that they must have been old hands at the game. The way they got in and opened the safe shows that. But there's one little thing that puzzles me. One of them was careless enough not to wear gloves, and I'm bothered if I know what he was trying to do. I've traced his finger-marks on the new varnish on the window-sashes in every one of the downstairs rooms. They are very distinctive ones too.'

'Right hand or left or both?' asked Eustace.

'Oh, right every time. That's the funny thing. He must have been a foolhardy fellow, and I rather think it was him that wrote that.' He took out a slip of paper from his pocket. 'That's what he wrote, sir: "I've got out, Eustace Borlsover, but I'll be back before long." Some jailbird just escaped, I suppose. It will make it all the easier for us to trace him. Do you know the writing, sir?'

'No,' said Eustace. 'It's not the writing of anyone I know.'

'I'm not going to stay here any longer,' said Eustace to Saunders at luncheon. 'I've got on far better during the last six months than I expected, but I'm not going to run the risk of seeing that thing again. I shall go up to town this afternoon. Get Morton to put my things together, and join me with the car at Brighton on the day after tomorrow. And bring the proofs of those two papers with you. We'll run over them together.'

'How long are you going to be away?'

'I can't say for certain, but be prepared to stay for some time. We've stuck to work pretty closely through the summer, and I for one need a holiday. I'll engage the rooms at Brighton. You'll find it best to break the journey at Hitchin. I'll wire to you there at the "Crown" to tell you the Brighton address.'

The house he chose at Brighton was in a terrace. He had been there before. It was kept by his old college gyp, a man of discreet silence, who was admirably partnered by an excellent cook. The rooms were on the first floor. The two bedrooms were at the back, and opened out of each other. 'Mr Saunders can have the smaller one, though it is the only one with a fire-place,' he said. 'I'll stick to the larger of the two, since it's got a bathroom adjoining. I wonder what time he'll arrive with the car.'

Saunders came about seven, cold and cross and dirty. 'We'll light the fire in the dining-room,' said Eustace, 'and get Prince to unpack some of the things while we are at dinner. What were the roads like?'

'Rotten. Swimming with mud, and a beastly cold wind against us all day. And this is July. Dear Old England!'

'Yes,' said Eustace, 'I think we might do worse than leave Old England for a few months.'

They turned in soon after twelve.

'You oughtn't to feel cold, Saunders,' said Eustace, 'when you can afford to sport a great fur-lined coat like this. You do yourself very well, all things considered. Look at those gloves, for instance. Who could possibly feel cold when wearing them?'

'They are far too clumsy, though, for driving. Try them on and see,' and he tossed them through the door on to Eustace's bed and went on with his unpacking. A minute later he heard a shrill cry of terror. 'Oh, Lord,' he heard, 'it's in the glove! Quick, Saunders quick!' Then came a smacking thud. Eustace had thrown it from him. 'I've chucked it into the bathroom,' he gasped; 'it's hit the wall and fallen into the bath. Come now, if you want to help,' Saunders, with a lighted candle in his hand, looked over the edge of the bath. There it was, old and maimed, dumb and blind, with a ragged hole in the middle, crawling, staggering, trying to creep up the slippery sides, only to fall back helpless.

'Stay there,' said Saunders. 'I'll empty a collar-box or something and we'll jam it in. It can't get out while I'm away.'

'Yes, it can,' shouted Eustace. 'It's getting out now; it's climbing up the plug-chain.—No, you brute, you filthy brute, you don't!—Come back, Saunders; it's getting away from me. I can't hold it; it's all slippery. Curse its claws! Shut the window, you idiot! It's got out!' There was the sound of something dropping on to the hard flag-stones below, and Eustace fell back fainting.

For a fortnight he was ill.

'I don't know what to make of it,' the doctor said to Saunders. 'I can only suppose that Mr Borlsover has suffered some great emotional shock. You had better let me send someone to help you nurse him. And by all means indulge that whim of his never to be left alone in the dark. I would keep a light burning all night, if I were you. But he *must* have more fresh air. It's perfectly absurd, this hatred of open windows.'

Eustace would have no one with him but Saunders. 'I don't want the other man,' he said. 'They'd smuggle it in somehow. I know they would.'

'Don't worry about it, old chap. This sort of thing can't go on indefinitely. You know I saw it this time as well as you. It wasn't half so active. It won't go on living much longer, especially after that fall. I heard it hit the flags myself. As soon as you're a bit stronger, we'll leave this place, not bag and baggage, but with only the clothes on our backs, so that it won't be able to hide anywhere. We'll escape it that way. We won't give any address, and we won't have any parcels sent after us. Cheer up, Eustace! You'll be well-enough to leave in a day or two. The doctor says I can take you out in a chair tomorrow.'

'What have I done?' asked Eustace. 'Why does it come after me? I'm no worse than other men. I'm no worse than you, Saunders; you know I'm not. It was you who was at the bottom of that dirty business in San Diego, and that was fifteen years ago.'

'It's not that, of course,' said Saunders. 'We are in the twentieth century, and even the parsons have dropped the idea of your old sins finding you out. Before you caught the hand in the library, it was filled with pure malevolence—to you and all mankind. After you spiked it through with that nail, it naturally forgot about other people and concentrated its attention on you. It was shut up in that safe, you know, for nearly six months. That gives plenty of time for thinking of revenge.'

Eustace Borlsover would not leave his room, but he thought there might be something in Saunders's suggestion of a sudden departure from Brighton. He began rapidly to regain his strength.

'We'll go on the first of September,' he said.

The evening of the thirty-first of August was oppressively warm. Though at midday the windows had been wide open, they had been shut an hour or so before dusk. Mrs Prince had long since ceased to wonder at the strange habits of the gentlemen on the first floor. Soon after their arrival she had been told to take down the heavy window curtains in the two bedrooms, and day by day the rooms had seemed to grow more bare. Nothing was left lying about.

'Mr Borlsover doesn't like to have any place where dirt can collect,' Saunders had said as an excuse. 'He likes to see into all the corners of the room.'

'Couldn't I open the window just a little?' he said to Eustace that evening. 'We're simply roasting in here, you know.'

'No, leave well alone. We're not a couple of boarding-school misses fresh from a course of hygiene lectures. Get the chess-board out.'

They sat down and played. At ten o'clock Mrs Prince came to the door with a note. 'I am sorry I didn't bring it before,' she said, 'but it was left in the letter-box.'

'Open it, Saunders, and see if it wants answering.'

It was very brief. There was neither address nor signature.

'Will eleven o'clock tonight be suitable for our last appointment?'

'Who is it from?' asked Borlsover.

'It was meant for me,' said Saunders. 'There's no answer, Mrs Prince,' and he put the paper into his pocket.

'A dunning letter from a tailor; I suppose he must have got wind of our leaving.'

It was a clever lie, and Eustace asked no more questions. They went on with their game.

On the landing outside Saunders could hear the grandfather's clock whispering the seconds, blurting out the quarter-hours.

'Check,' said Eustace. The clock struck eleven. At the same time there was a gentle knocking on the door; it seemed to come from the bottom panel.

'Who's there?' asked Eustace.

There was no answer.

'Mrs Prince, is that you?'

'She is up above,' said Saunders; 'I can hear her walking about the room.'

'Then lock the door; bolt it too. Your move, Saunders.'

While Saunders sat with his eyes on the chess-board, Eustace walked over to the window and examined the fastenings. He did the same in Saunders's room, and the bathroom. There were no doors between the three rooms, or he would have shut and locked them too.

'Now, Saunders,' he said, 'don't stay all night over your move. I've had time to smoke one cigarette already. It's bad to keep an invalid waiting. There's only one possible thing for you to do. What was that?'

'The ivy blowing against the window. There, it's your move now, Eustace.'

'It wasn't the ivy, you idiot! It was someone tapping at the window,' and he pulled up the blind. On the outer side of the window, clinging to the sash, was the hand.

'What is it that it's holding?'

'It's a pocket-knife. It's going to try to open the window by pushing back the fastener with the blade.'

'Well, let it try,' said Eustace. 'Those fasteners screw down; they can't be opened that way. Anyhow, we'll close the shutters. It's your move, Saunders; I've played.'

But Saunders found it impossible to fix his attention on the game. He could not understand Eustace, who seemed all at once to have lost his fear. 'What do you say to some wine?' he asked. 'You seem to be taking things coolly, but I don't mind confessing that I'm in a blessed funk.'

'You've no need to be. There's nothing supernatural about that hand, Saunders. I mean it seems to be governed by the laws of time and space. It's not the sort of thing that vanishes into thin air or slides through oaken doors. And since that's so, I defy it to get in here. We'll leave the place in the morning. I for one have bottomed the depths of fear. Fill your glass, man! The windows are all shuttered; the door is locked and bolted. Pledge me my Uncle Adrian! Drink, man! What are you waiting for?'

Saunders was standing with his glass half raised. 'It can get in,' he said hoarsely; 'it can get in. We've forgotten. There's the fireplace in my bedroom. It will come down the chimney.'

'Quick!' said Eustace, as he rushed into the other room; 'we haven't a minute to lose. What can we do? Light the fire, Saunders. Give me a match, quick!'

'They must be all in the other room. I'll get them.'

'Hurry, man, for goodness' sake! Look in the bookcase! Look in the bathroom! Here, come and stand here; I'll look.'

'Be quick!' shouted Saunders. 'I can hear something!'

'Then plug a sheet from your bed up the chimney. No, here's a match!' He had found one at last that had slipped into a crack in the floor.

'Is the fire laid? Good, but it may not burn. I know—the oil from that old reading-lamp and this cotton-wool. Now the match, quick! Pull the sheet away, you fool! We don't want it now.'

There was a great roar from the grate, as the flames shot up. Saunders had been a fraction of a second too late with the sheet. The oil had fallen on to it. It, too, was burning.

'The whole place will be on fire!' cried Eustace, as he tried to beat out the flames with a blanket. 'It's no good! I can't manage it. You must open the door, Saunders, and get help.'

Saunders ran to the door and fumbled with the bolts. The key was stiff in the lock. 'Hurry,' shouted Eustace, 'or the heat will be too much for me.' The key turned in the lock at last. For half a second Saunders stopped to look back. Afterwards he could never be quite sure as to what he had seen, but at the time he thought that something black and charred was creeping slowly, very slowly, from the mass of flames towards Eustace Borlsover. For a moment he thought of returning to his friend; but the noise and the smell of the burning sent him running down the passage, crying: 'Fire! Fire!' He rushed to the telephone to summon help, and then back to the bathroom—he should have thought of that before—for water. As he burst into the bedroom there came a scream of terror which ended suddenly, and then the sound of a heavy fall.

This is the story which I heard on successive Saturday evenings from the senior mathematical master at a second-rate suburban school. For Saunders has had to earn a living in a way which other men might reckon less congenial than his old manner of life. I had mentioned by chance the name of Adrian Borlsover, and wondered at the time why he changed the conversation with such unusual abruptness. A week later Saunders began to tell me something of his own history; sordid enough, though shielded with a reserve I could well understand, for it had to cover not only his failings, but those of a dead friend. Of the final tragedy he was at first especially loath to speak; and it was only gradually that I was able to piece together the narrative of the preceding pages. Saunders was reluctant to draw any conclusions. At one time he thought that the fingered beast had been animated by the spirit of Sigismund Borlsover, a sinister eighteenth-century ancestor, who, according to legend, built and worshipped in the ugly pagan temple that overlooked the lake. At another time Saunders believed the spirit to belong to a man whom Eustace had once employed as a laboratory assistant, 'a black-haired, spiteful little brute,' he said, 'who died cursing his doctor, because the fellow couldn't help him to live to settle some paltry score with Borlsover.'

From the point of view of direct contemporary evidence, Saunders's story is practically uncorroborated. All the letters mentioned in the narrative were destroyed, with the exception of the last note which Eustace received, or rather which he would have received, had not Saunders intercepted it. That I have seen myself. The handwriting was thin and shaky, the handwriting of an old man. I remember the Greek V was used in 'appointment'. A little thing that amused me at the time was that Saunders seemed to keep the note pressed between the pages of his Bible.

I had seen Adrian Borlsover once. Saunders I learnt to know well. It was by chance, however, and not by design, that I met a third person of the story, Morton, the butler. Saunders and I were walking in the Zoological Gardens one Sunday afternoon, when he called my attention to an old man who was standing before the door of the Reptile House.

'Why, Morton,' he said, clapping him on the back, 'how is the world treating you?'

'Poorly, Mr Saunders,' said the old fellow, though his face lighted up at the greeting. 'The winters drag terribly nowadays. There don't seem no summers or springs.'

'You haven't found what you were looking for, I suppose?'

'No, sir, not yet; but I shall some day. I always told them that Mr Borlsover kept some queer animals.'

'And what is he looking for?' I asked, when we had parted from him.

'A beast with five fingers,' said Saunders. 'This afternoon, since he has been in the Reptile House, I suppose it will be a reptile with a hand. Next week it will be a monkey with practically no body. The poor old chap is a born materialist.'

FIRST DAY IN THE LIFE OF A LION TRAINER

Patricia Bourne

'I shall be prepared to pay you twenty pounds a week as a learner if you can arrange to come to Paris, where my winter quarters and menagerie are, and let me see if I can teach you how to train lions and give a good performance with them.' The speaker was Mr Alfred Court, the world-famous wild-animal trainer, whose name was known all over Europe for his daring work.

'But what if I am no good?' I asked.

He smiled again. 'Then nor much time would be wasted, for I think we should discover that within ten seconds of your first entering a lion cage. I shall have to talk with your mother. Could you arrange that tomorrow? I have to leave for Berlin tomorrow night, so I am afraid a decision will have to be made quickly. Perhaps you will discuss it with your family this evening to prepare them. That is, of course, if you yourself are interested.'

'Yes, I am,' I said. 'I'm very interested in your offer.'

Needless to say, I telephoned mother and she, willing as always to advise and help me, came to the circus to hear what I was so excited about. Now, nobody else in our family had anything to do with the circus at all. My father had owned a respectable foreign-import business. He was also a very good sportsman. I was brought up mostly by a doting nanny and seldom spent holidays with my mother and father, but nearly always at nanny's home in the country near Clitheroe. There was a huge farm next door where my friends and I played 'circuses' with the big cart horses. During my school holidays I spent a lot of time on horseback.

I got myself into the theatrical business because Daddy died when I was eleven, and, as I got older, I saw that it was hard for mother to cope with everything and meet all the expenses.

I think the first shock I gave her was my job at the Blackpool Tower Ballet. From there I graduated to the Tower Circus. I knew, when I told her about my newest offer, that it was a shock to her. She'd got used to the idea of Colonel Lindsay and his whip act, in which I was partner, also the riding and swimming I did.

Now here I was, standing in my dressing-room in pale green velvet shorts, a satin blouse, a big sombrero hat on my head, ready for my entrance in the ring, begging her to let me go to Paris for a test to become a lion trainer! Sensible as always, she said yes, she would hear Mr Court's proposition the following day, but she was horribly afraid of such a dangerous job for me. And what would people say if she agreed to let me have a try?

I argued: 'Yes—but, Mother, I'll never be a really brilliant dancer, or a very good bareback rider.'

I am sure she thought: 'Why can't my daughter get a nice respectable job, something safe and sound?'

The following morning the meeting took place, and after many questions had been discussed, mostly about my safety, I received permission to go to Paris.

And now, here I was in a gaunt grey building in the Luna Park, Bois de Boulogne, Paris, feeling terribly afraid.

I had put on my riding-jodhpurs, and a blue corton sports-shirt, 'Wear something quiet,' Mr Court had warned me. 'something inconspicuous—and not a skirt, unless you want them to try and hook it away from you.'

The grooms had just finished putting up the 'runway'—a structure of steel bars like a very long winding toast rack—that linked the lion-wagon with the cage. Down this were to come the animals.

The lion cage itself stood empty, except for five red wooden stools that the lions were to sit on. The Paris day was chilly, but nothing was as cold as my stomach. I could feel icicles of fear inside me, quivering like chandelier glass, as I stood waiting for my first test in the cage. A test to see if I had courage, willpower, and enough sense to learn to handle the five lions now so peacefully asleep in their big blue and white wagons at the side of the cage.

Suddenly one big fellow got up, yawned, showing huge fangs, 'All the better to eat you with, my dear,' he seemed to say, as he rubbed his sides against the bars of his wagon as an old Billy goat does, sat down again and stared straight ahead.

And I, waiting, thought to myself: 'Soon, only too soon, I shall have to go into that big round steel cage and face both you and your pals, with no bars between us at all. How will you look at me then?' And I firmly wished myself back on the other side of the Channel.

Suddenly, Mr Court was there! I was soon to discover that he had a trick of appearing and disappearing quickly. He was also dressed in riding-breeches and a sports-shirt. He looked capable and distinguished.

First Day in the Life of a Lion Trainer 109

With a curt 'Good morning,' he said: 'Now, here is a light whip, made of Spanish cane, the only material in the world that makes a proper lion-whip.'

I took hold of the whip; it was very light.

'Also,' said Mr Court, 'you will carry a stick in your left hand, which I want you to please keep in front of you. Ready!' he said to the beast-man.

A long iron bar drew open the doors between the cages, and rising slowly, with bored expressions on their faces, the five lions came padding down the runway and into the big cage. Quietly they were ordered to their particular red stools: obediently they went.

So far, it was just like watching any circus-animal act. It didn't seem to have anything to do with me. Then Erik, the groom, was at my side.

'Ready,' he said, and it was a command rather than a question, as he untied the rope that loosely bound the door to the cage and Mr Court beckoned me in. I stepped inside, and heard the door clang behind me.

'Now,' he said quietly, 'I should like to say a few words to you, here by the door. It will give the animals a chance to look at you also.'

There was a strong smell of dung and ammonia and I became abruptly aware of five pairs of amber eyes, unwinking, each as big as a penny, staring at me. I had no idea how tall and tremendous a lion upon its circus stool is, until I came so close to them. Yet the feeling I had was not of fear. Surprisingly it was shyness. It was just as though I had blundered into a first-class compartment and was receiving the states of lorgnetted duchesses and their resentful gentlemen. Disdain, remote, cold, aloof, and inhuman—was the message that those yellow jungle-eyes held for me. I shivered, but stood quite still. Court, his eyes never leaving the lions, came closer to me.

'Now,' said my teacher, 'if you get into trouble—and only if, mark you—turn your whip round and use the handle, or the attacking animal will probably get a claw in the lash—and away goes your whip. If any animal attacks you, keep your stick in front of you and give the offender a sharp smack on the nose. If you are lucky then, he will probably turn away after having bitten savagely at your stick. Let him do this. He thinks a stick or whip in a person's hand is part of that person and that if he bites the stick it's really you he's biting; and as that does not seem to hurt ybu, he becomes discouraged. No use cracking a whip at an attacking lion. Might as well poke a straw at a madman.'

'Won't it hurt him?' I asked.

'Look,' said Court, 'a lion has no qualms of conscience. He isn't going to sit up nights worrying if he's killed or crippled somebody who's fond of him. But he does understand, if you stay in front of him, who's master. Go forward, forward, never backward, that's your morto. If you're cruel to a lion, he'll hate you. And if he hates you, he'll kill you some day. But even if he likes you, there comes a day when he will try to kill you. Nor for any sensible reason that a human could understand; maybe just because of a glint of sunlight on your thumbnail, or a whiff of sweat—and—even pretty lion trainers must sweat, believe me. Or a breeze in your hair, or the wrong edge in your voice one day when you've got a headache. Or for no reason at all, except he's a lion and you aren't. So, when the day arrives, it's no use saying: 'Lion remember me, I'm the person who feeds you.' A firm smack on the nose or rear quarters is the only argument he'll understand.'

'And isn't that being cruel?' I asked, hesitating.

I was told: 'A lioness boxes a cub's ears with a blow that would nearly crush your head. Remember, please, a lion's foreleg weighs almost as much as your entire body, my girl. Lions aren't pussy cats. And if a lion hits you, you will remember it all your life—if you have any left.

I thought to myself: He's putting things across very vividly, and I feel an awful fool here, so I'd better do the best I can not to look like one. Also, how the people at St Anne's would delight in saying: 'I told you so! Of course she's back! We knew she'd never manage that!'

'Come up close to the side of me,' said Court. 'We shall go over and talk to them.'

We walked slowly together to the lions, who continued to stare—not at him, but at me. One stirred a big paw restlessly.

'Go and tickle their noses gently with your whip,' I was told, 'and speak to them quietly by name. That first one is the lioness, Zulton.'

Earlier Mr Court had told me how Miss Violetta d'Argent, a French lion trainer who worked for him, had recently been badly mauled by a lioness named Zulton and had lost her nerve.

I did as I was told, thinking, 'You're the lady who did not like Violetta d'Argent.' Apparently she did not like me either, for she hissed vindictively and took a swing at my whip. What force behind that swing there was! I tried again. I poked her gently on her head and said: 'Good girl, Zulton.'

She stared down at me, looking as if she had the prim soul of an elderly school-mistress, which, of course, she had not. Zulton never did learn to like me, although I tried to make her do so. No, her one love was Alfred Court. For him she would roll over and purr.

The next stool was occupied by Belmonte, a huge African lion with a black mane and unusually long face, that made him look aristocratic and melancholy. His eyes were more green than amber and he stated at me curiously, with a sad hauteur.

I reached out hesitantly and tickled his whiskers as you do a cat's. He bated his teeth slowly, lifted open his enormous mouth and grunted 'Ooh-ah.' It sounded like a very deep-voiced parson clearing his throat. Somehow, I had a feeling he'd suddenly said something, and I do believe it was an expression of pleasure.

Suddenly there was a disturbance. The small, tawny lioness, Sevilla, had sprung from her heavy stool in a cloud of sawdust and seemed to be in mid-air, streaking towards me with claws outstretched. It was at that moment I realized that one must have eyes all over the place.

'Watch the others!' shouted Court.

Now I saw what a good teacher I had, for he placed himself with arms outstretched between me and the attacking lioness, and with a sharp clap of his hands—which is a trick known only to trainers—brought her to an abrupt srop. A sharp noise can often stop an animal bent on destruction much better than a hit. Otherwise, it probably would have been my last breathing moment. A reason no stranger is safe inside a cage of wild animals is the intense curiosity which often leads to these quick attacks.

Sevilla glared for a few seconds with malevolent jewel eyes at Mr Court, then gave me a long, silent glance and walked, with tail swishing, to her stool.

I had expected to be frightened. To my amazement, I discovered that instead of fear all I felt was anger. I marched straight over to the lioness and said passionately:

'You naughty girl! How dare you!'

I think she sensed my anger, and I suddenly had a feeling that these animals were like any others, only a little more dangerous. Show them you are afraid, and they will surely see it and take advantage. I stood right in front of her, looking into her eyes and thinking: 'Yes, just you dare try that again, lady!'

And slowly her ears drooped and her big face became hangdog like and she blew down her nose in what was obviously embarrassment. Later, she was to become one of my best show-lions. I did not dare show it, but she looked a darling after her defeat.

I looked round the cage then and saw all the other four pairs of amber eyes watching me and the faces held up, as if startled. They all looked positively shocked. I thought the big paws of Sevilla were actually trembling.

I did not know then that a lion will sometimes quiver when he is contemplating villainy; also that he never roars when he is angry, only when he is hungry or bored; that in a few months I was to see Granada kill another lioness before my eyes, have my leg ripped in Spain, and be forced to stand staring, locked in a battle of wills—with another lion named Nero, commanding him to be still, while his claw was actually hooked in my finger.

'Don't forget to pay your respects to Guieto and Granada,' said Mr Court.

As I slowly approached Guieto he bated, I should imagine, every tooth in his mouth, but turned his head from side to side as I stroked his whiskers with the butt end of my whip. Granada sat quite still. She looked a queer character: frightfully clean coat—rather, I thought, like the matron of a hospital—only the little cap was missing from her head.

After I had, under Mr Court's instructions, fed each lion with little bits of meat from a pointed stick and talked to them as I was doing so—trying to win their confidence a little—we backed towards the door. Erik opened it just enough for me to squeeze through.

Mr Court sent my little party of five friends back to their living quarters. Away they scuttled up the runway, glad to be rid of us, also knowing it was nearing lunch time.

'So far, so good,' said Mr Court. 'Now comes the rather messier side. Come round the side of the lam wagon. Martin,' he called to another beast-man, 'bring the meat, and lend the lady an overall and the knife.'

Martin did as he was told.

I looked on in horror as a huge piece of horse-meat was placed by hooks on the wooden table at the side of the end wagon.

'Put the coat on, take up the knife and let me see if you can cut up five nice big steaks,' I was told. 'Also, dissect all small bone-splinters.'

'How big a steak?' I asked.

'Oh, like this,' said Mr Court, stretching his hands to show the size. 'Actually they eat about fifteen pounds a day each, but we don't weigh, we go with our eye measurement and judgement. The first is for Zulton; she likes all meat. Belmonte likes meat and a bone, so you'll probably need the axe too.'

I felt the grooms were silent, but laughing a little. Well, I'd show them! I took the sharp knife and started to cut. The meat felt very slippery and I admit I did not like holding it one bit.

'You see,' said Court, 'a lion trainer has many jobs to perform, and many responsibilities, too. It's not as easy as people imagine, to have the training and care of animals, especially wild ones.'

I quite believed this when, with a groom's help, I had cut

five nice steaks out and they were laid neatly side by side on the scrubbed board. By this time the wagons were swaying with a peculiar rhythm as the hungry family paced back and forth, waiting for lunch to be served.

'Now,' said my teacher, 'you will take the iron bar and open each little door in front of each wagon in turn. Always see that the safety-chain is in place, so that the door opens only so far and no farther. It's just enough for a groom to get the meat through on a fork. And please keep at a distance, or they might swing out and catch your arm instead of the meat.'

I took the bar with the little crook at the end and we approached the first cage. The rattling inside grew louder, with excitement and anticipation. However, I managed to insert the tip of the bar, as I was shown, into the first door and, on the word 'lift', I pushed. The door shot up. At the same second the groom inserted the fork with the meat, which was seized with tremendous force and immediately examined.

It all seemed to go smoothly: I suddenly had a picture in my head of a first-class dining-car on a train where we were the waiters, supplying the diners with their dinner, providing the quickest possible service.

Then I waited with great apprehension to hear my fate and was told, 'so far, so good,' and that this afternoon I should be tried out to see how long it would take me to learn to use a whip in the correct and safe way. I also learnt that, if everything proceeded to plan, I should give my first performance before the public in three weeks' time.

I was so happy I could have hugged my five new friends. Instead, I had to be content watching the grooms putting in the dry, clean straw for the night.

ESCAPE FROM JAVA

Ruskin Bond

> *'No one, it seemed, was interested in defending java, only in getting out as fast as possible.'*

It all happened within the space of a few days. The cassia tree had barely come into flower when the first bombs fell on Batavia (now called Jakarta) and the bright pink blossoms lay scattered over the wreckage in the streets.

News had reached us that Singapore had fallen to the Japanese. My father said: 'I expect it won't be long before they take Java. With the British defeated, how can the Dutch be expected to win!' He did not mean to be critical of the Dutch; he knew they did not have the backing of an Empire such as Britain then had. Singapore had been called the Gibraltar of the East. After its surrender there could only be retreat, a vast exodus of Europeans from South-East Asia.

It was World War II. What the Javanese thought about the war is now hard for me to say, because I was only nine at the time and knew little of worldly matters. Most people knew they would be exchanging their Dutch rulers for Japanese rulers; but there were also many who spoke in terms of freedom for Java when the war was over.

Our neighbour, Mr Hartono, was one of those who looked ahead to a time when Java, Sumatra and the other islands would make up one independent nation. He was a college professor and spoke Dutch, Chinese, Javanese and a little English. His son, Sono, was about my age. He was the only boy I knew who could talk to me in English, and as a result we spent a lot of time together. Our favourite pastime was flying kites in the park.

The bombing soon put an end to kite-flying. Air raid alerts sounded at all hours of the day and night, and although in the beginning most of the bombs fell near the docks, a couple of miles from where we lived, we had to stay indoors. If the planes sounded very near, we dived under beds or tables. I don't remember if there were any trenches. Probably there hadn't been time for trench digging, and now there was time only for digging graves. Events had moved all too swiftly, and everyone (except of course the Javanese) was anxious to get away from Java.

'When are you going?' asked Sono, as we sat on the veranda steps in a pause between air raids.

'I don't know,' I said. 'It all depends on my father.'

'My father says the Japs will be here in a week. And if you're still here then, they'll put you to work building a railway.'

'I wouldn't mind building a railway,' I said.

'But they won't give you enough to eat. Just rice with worms in it. And if you don't work properly they'll shoot you.'

'They do that to soldiers,' I said. 'We're civilians.'

'They do it to civilians, too,' said Sono.

What were my father and I doing in Batavia, when our home had been first in India and then in Singapore? He worked for a firm dealing in rubber, and six months earlier he had been sent to Batavia to open a new office in partnership with a Dutch business house. Although I was so young, I accompanied my father almost everywhere. My mother had died when I was very small, and my father had always looked after me. After the war was over he was going to take me to England.

'Are we going to win the war?' I asked.

'It doesn't look it from here,' he said.

No, it didn't look as though we were winning. Standing at the docks with my father, I watched the ships arrive from Singapore crowded with refugees—men, women and children all living on the decks in the tropical sun; they looked pale and worn-out and worried. They were on their way to Colombo or Bombay. No one came ashore at Batavia. It wasn't British territory; it was Dutch, and everyone knew it wouldn't be Dutch for long.

'Aren't we going too?' I asked. 'Sono's father says the Japs will be here any day.'

'We've still got a few days,' said my father. He was a short, stocky man, who seldom got excited. If he was worried, he didn't show it. 'I've got to wind up a few business matters, and then we'll be off.'

'How will we go? There's no room for us on those ships.'

'There certainly isn't. But we'll find a way, lad, don't worry.'

I didn't worry. I had complete confidence in my father's ability to find a way out of difficulties. He used to say, 'Every problem has a solution hidden away somewhere, and if only you look hard enough you will find it.'

There were British soldiers in the streets but they did not make us feel much safer. They were just waiting for troop ships to come and take them away. No one, it seemed, was interested in defending Java, only in getting out as fast as possible.

Although the Dutch were unpopular with the Javanese people, there was no ill-feeling against individual Europeans. I could walk safely through the streets. Occasionally small boys in the crowded Chinese quarter would point at me and shout, '*Orang Balandi* (Dutchman!)', but they did so in good humour, and I didn't know the language well enough to stop and explain that the English weren't Dutch. For them, all white people were the same, and understandably so.

My father's office was in the commercial area, along the canal banks. Our two-storied house, about a mile away, was an old building with a roof of red tiles and a broad balcony which had stone dragons at either end. There were flowers in the garden almost all the year round. If there was anything in Batavia more regular than the bombing, it was the rain, which came pattering down on the roof and on the banana fronds almost every afternoon. In the hot and steamy atmosphere of Java, the rain was always welcome.

There were no anti-aircraft guns in Batavia—at least we never heard any—and the Jap bombers came over at will, dropping their bombs by daylight. Sometimes bombs fell in the town. One day the building next to my father's office received a direct hit and tumbled into the river. A number of office workers were killed.

One day Sono said, 'The bombs are falling on Batavia, not in the countryside. Why don't we get cycles and ride out of town?'

I fell in with the idea at once. After the morning all-clear had sounded, we mounted our cycles and rode out of town. Mine was a hired cycle, but Sono's was his own. He'd had it since the age of five, and it was constantly in need of repairs. 'The soul has gone out of it,' he used to say.

Our fathers were at work; Sono's mother had gone out to do her shopping (during air-raids she took shelter under the most convenient shop-counter) and wouldn't be back for at least an hour. We expected to be back before lunch.

We were soon out of town, on a road that passed through rice fields, pineapple orchards and cinchona plantations. On our right lay dark green hills; on our left, groves of coconut palms and, beyond them, the sea. Men and women were working in the rice fields, knee-deep in mud, their broad-brimmed hats protecting them from the fierce sun. Here and there a buffalo wallowed in a pool of brown water, while a naked boy lay stretched out on the animal's broad back.

We took a bumpy track through the palms. They grew right down to the edge of the sea. Leaving our cycles on the shingle, we ran down a smooth, sandy beach and into the shallow water.

'Don't go too far in,' warned Sono. 'There may be sharks about.'

Wading in amongst the rocks, we searched for interesting shells, then sat down on a large rock and looked out to sea, where a sailing ship moved placidly on the crisp blue waters. It was difficult to imagine that half the world was at war, and that Batavia, two or three miles away, was right in the middle of it.

On our way home we decided to take a shortcut through the rice fields, but soon found that our tires got bogged down in the soft mud. This delayed our return; and to make things worse, we got the roads mixed up and reached an area of the town that seemed unfamiliar. We had barely entered the outskirts when the siren sounded, to be followed soon after by the drone of approaching aircraft.

'Should we get off our cycles and take shelter somewhere?' I called out.

'No, let's race home!' shouted Sono. 'The bombs won't fall here.'

But he was wrong. The planes flew in very low. Looking up

for a moment, I saw the sun blotted out by the sinister shape of a Jap fighter-bomber. We pedalled furiously; but we had barely covered fifty yards when there was a terrific explosion on our right, behind some houses. The shock sent us spinning across the road. We were flung from our cycles. And the cycles, still propelled by the blast, crashed into a wall.

I felt a stinging sensation in my hands and legs, as though scores of little insects had bitten me. Tiny droplets of blood appeared here and there on my flesh. Sono was on all fours, crawling beside me, and I saw that he too had the same small scratches on his hands and forehead, made by tiny shards of flying glass.

We were quickly on our feet, and then we began running in the general direction of our homes. The twisted cycles lay forgotten on the road.

'Get off the street, you two!' shouted someone from a window; but we weren't going to stop running until we got home. And we ran faster than we'd ever run in our lives.

My father and Sono's parents were themselves running about the street, calling for us, when we came rushing around the corner and tumbled into their arms.

'Where have you been?'

'What happened to you?'

'How did you get those cuts?'

All superfluous questions; but before we could recover our breath and start explaining, we were bundled into our respective homes. My father washed my cuts and scratches, dabbed at my face and legs with iodine—ignoring my yelps—and then stuck plaster all over my face.

Sono and I had both had a fright, and we did not venture far from the house again.

That night my father said: 'I think we'll able to leave in a day or two.'

'Has another ship come in?'

'No.'

'Then how are we going? By plane?'

'Wait and see, lad. It isn't settled yet. But we won't be able to take much with us—just enough to fill a couple of traveling bags.'

'What about the stamp collection?' I asked.

My father's stamp collection was quite valuable, and filled several volumes.

'I'm afraid we'll have to leave most of it behind,' he said. 'Perhaps Mr Hartono will keep it for me, and when the war is over—if it's ever over we'll come back for it.'

'But we can take one or two albums with us, can't we?'

'I'll take one. There'll be room for one. Then if we're short of money in Bombay, we can sell the stamps.'

'Bombay? That's in India. I thought we were going back to England.'

'First we must go to India.'

The following morning I found Sono in the garden, patched up like me, and with one foor in a bandage. But he was as cheerful as ever and gave me his usual wide grin.

'We're leaving tomorrow,' I said.

The grin left his face.

'I will be sad when you go,' he said. 'But I will be glad too, because then you will be able to escape from the Japs.'

'After the war, I'll come back.'

'Yes, you must come back. And then, when we are big, we will go round the world together. I want to see England and America and Africa and India and Japan. I want to go everywhere.'

'We can't go everywhere.'

'Yes, we can. No one can stop us!'

We had to be up very early the next morning. Our bags had been packed late at night. We were taking a few clothes, some of my father's business papers, a pair of binoculars, one stamp album and several bars of chocolate. I was pleased about the stamp album and the chocolates, but I had to give up several of my treasures—favourite books, the gramophone and records, and old Samurai sword, a train set and a dartboard. The only consolation was that Sono, and not a stranger, would have them.

In the first faint light of dawn a truck drew up in front of the house. It was driven by a Dutch businessman, Mr Hookens, who worked with my father. Sono was already at the gate, waiting to say good-bye.

'I have a present for you,' he said.

He took me by the hand and pressed a smooth, hard object into my palm. I grasped it and then held it up against the light. It was a beautiful little seahorse, carved out of pale blue jade.

'It will bring you luck,' said Sono.

'Thank you,' I said. 'I will keep it forever.'

And I slipped the little sea horse into my pocket.

'In you get, lad,' said my father, and I got up on the front seat between him and Mr Hookens.

As the truck started up, I turned to wave to Sono. He was sitting on his garden wall, grinning at me. He called out: 'We will go everywhere, and no one can stop us!'

He was still waving when the truck took us round the bend at the end of the road.

We drove through the still, quiet streets of Batavia, occasionally passing burnt-out trucks and shattered buildings. Then we left the sleeping city far behind and were climbing into the forested hills. It had rained during the night, and when the sun came up over the green hills, it twinkled and glittered on the broad wet leaves. The light in the forest changed from dark green to greenish gold, broken here and there by the flaming red or orange of a trumpet-shaped blossom. It was impossible to know the names of all those fantastic plants! The road had been cut through dense tropical forest, and on either side, the trees jostled each other, hungry for the sun; but they were chained together by the liana creepers and vines that fed upon the same struggling trees.

Occasionally a jelarang, a large javan squirrel, frightened by the passing of the truck, leapt through the trees before disappearing into the depths of the forest. We saw many birds: peacocks, junglefowl, and once, standing majestically at the side of the road, a crowned pigeon, its great size and splendid crest making it a striking object even at a distance. Mr Hookens slowed down so that we could look at the bird. It bowed its head so that its crest swept the ground; then it emitted a low hollow boom rather than the call of a turkey.

When we came to a small clearing, we stopped for breakfast. Butterflies, black, green and gold, flitted across the clearing. The silence of the forest was broken only by the drone of airplanes, Japanese Zeros heading for Batavia on another raid. I thought about Sono, and wondered what he would be doing at home: probably trying out the gramophone!

We ate boiled eggs and drank tea from a thermos, then got back into the truck and resumed our journey.

I must have dozed off soon after because the next thing I remember is that we were going quite fast down a steep, winding road, and in the distance I could see a calm blue lagoon.

'We've reached the sea again,' I said.

'That's right,' said my father. 'But we're now nearly a hundred miles from Batavia, in another part of the island. You're looking out over the Sunda Straits.'

Then he pointed towards a shimmering white object resting on the waters of the lagoon.

'There's our plane,' he said.

'A seaplane!' I exclaimed. 'I never guessed. Where will it take us?'

'To India, I hope. There aren't many other places left to go to!'

It was a very old seaplane, and no one, not even the captain—the pilot was called the captain—could promise that it would take off. Mr Hookens wasn't coming with us; he said the plane would be back for him the next day. Besides my father and me, there were four other passengers, and all but one were Dutch. The odd man out was a Londoner, a motor mechanic who'd been left behind in Java when his unit was evacuated. (He told us later that he'd fallen asleep at a bar in the Chinese quarter, waking up some hours after his regiment had moved off!) He looked rather scruffy. He'd lost the top button of his shirt, but, instead of leaving his collar open, as we did, he'd kept it together with a large safety pin, which thrust itself out from behind a bright pink tie.

'It's a relief to find you here, guvnor,' he said, shaking my father by the hand. 'Knew you for a Yorkshireman the minute I set eyes on you. It's the *song-fried* that does it, if you know what I mean.' (He meant *sang-froid*, French for a 'cool look'.) 'And here I was, with all these flippin' forriners, and me not knowing a word of what they've been yattering about. Do you think this old tub will get us back to Blighty?'

'It does look a bit shaky,' said my father. 'One of the first flying boats, from the looks of it. If it gets us to Bombay, that's far enough.'

'Anywhere out of Java's good enough for me,' said our new companion. 'The name's Muggeridge.'

'Pleased to know you, Mr Muggeridge,' said my father, 'I'm Bond. This is my son.'

Mr Muggeridge rumpled my hair and favoured me with a large wink.

The captain of the seaplane was beckoning to us to join him in a small skiff which was about to take us across a short stretch of water to the seaplane.

'Here we go,' said Mr Muggeridge. 'Say your prayers and keep your fingers crossed.'

The seaplane was a long time getting airborne. It had to make several runs before it finally took off; then, lurching drunkenly, it rose into the clear blue sky.

'For a moment I thought we were going to end up in the briny,' said Mr Muggeridge, untying his seat belt. 'And talkin' of fish, I'd give a week's wages for a plate of fish an' chips and a pint of beer.'

'I'll buy you a beer in Calcutta,' said my father.

'Have an egg,' I said, remembering we still had some boiled eggs in one of the traveling bags.

'Thanks, mate,' said Mr Muggeridge, accepting an egg with alacrity. 'A real egg, too! I've been livin' on egg powder these last six months. That's what they give you in the army. And it ain't hens' eggs they make it from, let me tell you. It's either gulls' or turtles' eggs!'

'No,' said my father with a straight face. 'Snakes' eggs.'

Mr Muggeridge turned a delicate shade of green; but he soon recovered his poise, and for about an hour kept talking about almost everything under the sun, including Churchill, Hitler, Roosevelt, Mahatma Gandhi and Betty Grable. (The last-named was famous for her beautiful legs.) He would have gone on talking all the way to India had he been given a chance; but suddenly a shudder passed through the old plane, and it began lurching again.

'I think an engine is giving trouble,' said my father.

When I looked through the small glassed-in window, it seemed as though the sea was rushing up to meet us.

The co-pilot entered the passenger cabin and said something in Dutch. The passengers looked dismayed, and immediately began fastening their seat belts.

'Well, what did the blighter say?' asked Mr Muggeridge.

'I think he's going to have to ditch the plane,' said my father, who knew enough Dutch to get the gist of anything that was said.

'Down in the drink!' exclaimed Mr Muggeridge. 'Gawd 'elp us! And how far are we from India, guv?'

'A few hundred miles,' said my father.

'Can you swim, mate?' asked Mr Muggeridge looking at me.

'Yes,' I said. 'But not all the way to Bombay. How far can you swim?'

'The length of a bathtub,' he said.

'Don't worry,' said my father. 'Just make sure your life jacket's properly tied.'

We looked to our life jackets; my father checked mine twice, making sure that it was properly fastened.

The pilot had now cut both engines, and was bringing the plane down in a circling movement. But he couldn't control the speed, and it was tilting heavily to one side. Instead of landing smoothly on its belly, it came down on a wing rip, and this caused the plane to swivel violently around in the choppy sea. There was a terrific jolt when the plane hit the water, and if it hadn't been for the seat belts we'd have been flung from our seats. Even so, Mr Muggeridge struck his head against the seat in front, and he was now holding a bleeding nose and using some shocking language.

As soon as the plane came to a standstill, my father undid my seat belt. There was no time to lose. Water was already filling the cabin, and all the passengers—except one, who was dead in his seat with a broken neck—were scrambling for the exit hatch. The co-pilot pulled a lever and the door fell away to reveal high waves slapping against the sides of the stricken plane.

Holding me by the hand, my father was leading me towards the exit.

'Quick lad,' he said. 'We won't stay afloat for long.'

'Give us a hand!' shouted Mr Muggeridge, still struggling with his life jacket. 'First this bloody bleedin' nose, and now something's gone and stuck.'

My father helped him fix his life jacket, then pushed him out of the door ahead of us.

As we swam away from the seaplane (Mr Muggeridge splashing furiously alongside us), we were aware of the other passengers in the water. One of them shouted to us in Dutch to follow him.

We swam after him towards the dinghy, which had been released the moment we hit the water. That yellow dinghy, bobbing about on the waves, was as welcome as land.

All who had left the plane managed to climb into the dinghy. We were seven altogether—a tight fit. We had hardly settled down in the well of the dinghy when Mr Muggeridge, still holding his nose, exclaimed: 'There she goes!' And as we looked on helplessly, the seaplane sank swiftly and silently beneath the waves.

The dinghy had shipped a lot of water, and soon everyone was busy bailing it out with mugs (there were a couple in the dinghy), hats and bare hands. There was a light swell, and every now and then water would roll in again and half fill the dinghy. But within half-an-hour we had most of the water out, and then it was possible to take turns, two men doing the bailing while the others rested. No one expected me to do this work, but I took a hand anyway, using my father's sola topi for the purpose.

'Where are we?' asked one of the passengers.

'A long way from anywhere,' said another.

'There must be a few islands in the Indian Ocean.'

'But we may be at sea for days before we come to one of them.'

'Days or even weeks,' said the captain. 'Let us look at our supplies.'

The dinghy appeared to be fairly well provided with emergency rations: biscuits, raisins, chocolates (we'd lost our own), and enough water to last a week. There was also a first-aid box, which was put to immediate use, as Mr Muggeridge's nose needed attention. A few others had cuts and bruises. One of the passengers had received a hard knock on the head and appeared to be suffering from loss of memory. He had no idea how we happened to be drifting about in the middle of the Indian Ocean; he was convinced that we were on a pleasure cruise a few miles off Batavia.

The unfamiliar motion of the dinghy, as it rose and fell in the troughs between the waves, resulted in almost everyone getting seasick. As no one could eat anything, a day's rations were saved.

The sun was very hot, but my father covered my head with

a large spotted handkerchief. He'd always had a fancy for bandana handkerchiefs with yellow spots, and seldom carried fewer than two on his person; so he had one for himself too. The sola-topi, well soaked in seawater, was being used by Mr Muggeridge.

It was only when I had recovered to some extent from my seasickness that I remembered the valuable stamp album, and sat up, exclaiming, 'The stamps! Did you bring the stamp album, Dad?'

He shook his head ruefully. 'It must be at the bottom of the sea by now,' he said. 'But don't worry, I kept a few rare stamps in my wallet.' And looking pleased with himself, he tapped the pocket of his bush shirt.

The dinghy drifted all day, with no one having the least idea where it might be taking us.

'Probably going round in circles,' said Mr Muggeridge pessimistically.

There was no compass and no sail, and paddling wouldn't have got us far even if we'd had paddles; we could only resign ourselves to the whims of the current and hope it would take us towards land or at least to within hailing distance of some passing ship.

The sun went down like an overripe tomato dissolving slowly in the sea. The darkness pressed down on us. It was a moonless night, and all we could see was the white foam on the crests of the waves. I lay with my head on my father's shoulder, and looked up at the stars which glittered in the remote heavens.

'Perhaps your friend Sono will look up at the sky tonight and see those same stars,' said my father. 'The world isn't so big after all.'

'All the same, there's a lot of sea around us,' said Mr Muggeridge from out of the darkness.

Remembering Sono, I put my hand in my pocket and was reassured to feel the smooth outline of the jade seahorse.

'I've still got Sono's seahorse,' I said, showing it to my father.

'Keep it carefully,' he said. 'It may bring us luck.'

'Are seahorses lucky?'

'Who knows? But he gave it to you with love, and love is like a prayer. So keep it carefully.'

I didn't sleep much that night. I don't think anyone slept. No one spoke much either, except of course Mr Muggeridge, who kept muttering something about cold beer and salami.

I didn't feel so sick the next day. By ten o'clock I was quite hungry; but breakfast consisted of two biscuits, a piece of chocolate, and a little drinking water. It was another hot day, and we were soon very thirsty, but everyone agreed that we should ration ourselves strictly.

Two or three still felt ill, but the others, including Mr Muggeridge, had recovered their appetites and normal spirits, and there was some discussion about the prospects of being picked up.

'Are there any distress-rockets in the dinghy?' asked my father. 'If we see a ship or a plane, we can fire a rocket and hope to be spotted. Otherwise there's not much chance of our being seen from a distance.'

A thorough search was made in the dinghy, but there were no rockets.

'Someone must have used them last Guy Fawkes Day,' commented Mr Muggeridge.

'They don't celebrate Guy Fawkes Day in Holland,' said my father. 'Guy Fawkes was an Englishman.'

'Ah,' said Mr Muggeridge, nor in the least put out. 'I've always said, most great men are Englishmen. And what did this chap Guy Fawkes do?'

'Tried to blow up Parliament,' said my father.

That afternoon we saw our first sharks. They were enormous creatures, and as they glided backward and forward under the boat it seemed they might hit and capsize us. They went away for some time, but returned in the evening.

At night, as I lay half-asleep beside my father, I felt a few drops of water strike my face. At first I thought it was the sea spray; but when the sprinkling continued, I realized that it was raining lightly.

'Rain!' I shouted, sitting up. 'It's raining!'

Everyone woke up and did their best to collect water in mugs, hats or other containers. Mr Muggeridge lay back with his mouth open, drinking the rain as it fell.

'This is more like it,' he said. 'You can have all the sun an' sand in the world. Give me a rainy day in England!'

But by early morning the clouds had passed, and the day turned out to be even hotter than the previous one. Soon we were all red and raw from sunburn. By midday even Mr Muggeridge was silent. No one had the energy to talk.

Then my father whispered, 'Can you hear a plane, lad?'

I listened carefully, and above the hiss of the waves I heard what sounded like the distant drone of a plane; but it must have been very far away, because we could not see it. Perhaps it was flying into the sun, and the glare was too much for our sore eyes; or perhaps we'd just imagined the sound.

Then the Dutchman who'd lost his memory thought he saw land, and kept pointing towards the horizon and saying, 'That's Batavia, I told you we were close to shore!' No one else saw anything. So my father and I weren't the only ones imagining things.

Said my father, 'It only goes to show that a man can see what he wants to see, even if there's nothing to be seen!

The sharks were still with us. Mr Muggeridge began to resent them. He took off one of his shoes and hurled it at the nearest shark; but the big fish ignored the shoe and swam on after us.

'Now, if your leg had been in that shoe, Mr Muggeridge, the shark might have accepted it,' observed my father.

'Don't throw your shoes away,' said the captain. 'We might land on a deserted coastline and have to walk hundreds of miles!'

A light breeze sprang up that evening, and the dinghy moved more swiftly on the choppy water.

'At last we're moving forward,' said the captain.

'In circles,' said Mr Muggeridge.

But the breeze was refreshing; it cooled our burning limbs, and helped us to get some sleep. In the middle of the night I woke up feeling very hungry.

'Are you all right?' asked my father, who had been awake all the time.

'Just hungry,' I said.

'And what would you like to eat?'

'Oranges!'

He laughed. 'No oranges on board. But I kept a piece of my chocolate for you. And there's a little water, if you're thirsty.'

I kept the chocolate in my mouth for a long time, trying to make it last. Then I sipped a little water.

'Arent you hungry?' I asked.

'Ravenous! I could eat a whole turkey. When we get to Calcutta or Madras or Colombo, or wherever it is we get to, we'll go to the best restaurant in town and eat like—like—'

'Like shipwrecked sailors!' I said.

'Exactly.'

'Do you think we'll ever get to land, Dad?'

'I'm sure we will. You're not afraid, are you?'

'No. Not as long as you're with me.'

Next morning to everyone's delight, we saw seagulls. This was a sure sign that land couldn't be far away; but a dinghy could take days to drift a distance of thirty or forty miles. The birds wheeled noisily above the dinghy. Their cries were the first familiar sounds we had heard for three days and three nights, apart from the wind and the sea and our own weary voices.

The sharks had disappeared, and that too was an encouraging sign. They didn't like the oil slicks that were appearing in the water.

But presently the gulls left us, and we feared we were drifting away from land.

'Circles,' repeated Mr Muggeridge. 'Circles.'

We had sufficient food and water for another week at sea; but no one even wanted to think about spending another week at sea.

The sun was a ball of fire. Our water ration wasn't sufficient to quench our thirst. By noon, we were without much hope or energy.

My father had his pipe in his mouth. He didn't have any tobacco, but he liked holding the pipe between his teeth. He said it prevented his mouth from getting too dry.

The sharks came back.

Mr Muggeridge removed his other shoe and threw it at them.

'Nothing like a lovely wet English summer,' he mumbled.

I fell asleep in the well of the dinghy, my father's large handkerchief spread over my face. The yellow spots on the cloth seemed to grow into enormous revolving suns.

When I woke up, I found a huge shadow hanging over us. At first I thought it was a cloud. But it was a shifting shadow. My father took the handkerchief from my face and said, 'You can wake up now, lad. We'll be home and dry soon.'

A fishing boat was beside us, and the shadow came from its wide flapping sail. A number of bronzed, smiling, chattering fishermen—Burmese, as we discovered later—were gazing down at us from the deck of their boat.

A few days later my father and I were in Calcutta.

My father sold his rare stamps for over a thousand rupees, and we were able to live in a comfortable hotel. Mr Muggeridge was flown back to England. Later we got a postcard from him, saying the English rain was awful!

'And what about us?' I asked. 'Aren't we going back to England?'

'Not yet,' said my father. 'You'll be going to a boarding school in Simla, until the war's over.'

'But why should I leave you?' I asked.

'Because I've joined the R.A.F.,' he said. 'Don't worry, I'm being posted in Delhi. I'll be able to come up to see you sometimes.'

A week later I was on a small train which went chugging up the steep mountain track to Simla. Several Indian, Ango-Indian and English children tumbled around in the compartment. I felt quite out of place among them, as though I had grown out of their pranks. But I wasn't unhappy. I knew my father would be coming to see me soon. He'd promised me some books, a pair of rollerskates, and a cricket bat, just as soon as he got his first month's pay.

Meanwhile, I had the jade seahorse which Sono had given me. And I have it with me today.

HUNTERS OF SOULS

Augustus Somerville

During a long period of service in the Survey Department of the Government of India, I have had occasions, to visit many of the remotest parts of India, away from the beaten tracks and devoid of those forms and amenities of civilization that an average traveller learns to expect.

It was on one of these excursions that I came across an extraordinary tribe living in the heart of the mountain fastnesses of Chhota Nagpur. These people who call themselves Bhills, but who, I have reason to suspect from their colour, language and facial expressions, are closely related to the Sontal and Ghond tribes, are a nomadic, semi-barbaric race living exclusively on wild animals, in the snaring and trapping of which they are experts, and also on their reputation as 'Soul Catchers'. In this last extraordinary avocation I was most interested, but could glean no information from the natives themselves until one day I had an opportunity of watching a 'Soul Catcher' at work.

Early in October. 1908, I received orders to survey a large section of forest land in the Palamu District. Certain wise-acres had discovered traces of minerals, such as mica, coal, etc., in the neighbourhood and were making tentative offers for the purchase of a large tract of this land, with mining rights thrown in. A wide-awake government, hearing that I had a mining engineer's certificate attached to the many credentials that secured me this position, decided to send me down to survey the land, and incidentally report on its possibilities as a mining area.

I will hasten over the first part of the journey as uninteresting, but once at Daltonganj, a small station on the extreme end of the only decent motoring road in the district, I found myself on the brink of the unknown.

Next morning I procured a hand-cart for the transport of my tent, guns, ammunition, etc., and with two servants and a native guide, set out for the interior.

The only road was a rough cart track, which after we had followed for about six miles, disappeared in the impenetrable undergrowth through which we were compelled to travel; abandoning the cart, we bundled the tent and accessories into three packs, which my two servants and the guide carried, and shouldering my rifle myself, set out on the 30-mile trek that would eventually bring us to the village of the Soul Catchers.

That night we camped on the edge of the jungle, near the banks of a small stream. In a short time we had the tent erected and a good fire blazing merrily. Dangerous animals were numerous in the district, and after a good dinner, I turned in with my rifle fully loaded on the cot besides me.

Nothing untoward occurred that night, but in the early hours of the morning, the servants awoke me with the disquieting information that our guide had disappeared.

Needless to say, I took this information very seriously. To be without a guide in that wilderness of unchartered forest and impenetrable bush was alarming enough, but what worried me most was that I had supplies only for a couple of days, and the possibilities of locating the village without a guide was remote enough to depress the most sanguine of explorers.

I will never forget the three days we wandered in that forest. It was one of the most awful experiences I have ever had.

From the onset, I had determined to travel light and so abandoned the tent and other heavy accessories. My survey instruments, I buried securely in the vicinity of a large pepul tree, marking the spot with several heavy boulders from the adjoining stream, then carrying only our food, guns and ammunition, set out for the nearest human habitation.

Directing myself solely with my pocket compass, I travelled due south-east—the direction we were taking prior to the guide's disappearance. Of beaten tracks there were none, but hitherto we had managed to avoid the worst sections of the forest fairly successfully. Bereft of the experience and woodcraft of our guide, we blundered into all manner of pitfalls, and on several occasions found ourselves in thick masses of undergrowth composed almost entirely of stunted plum bushes fairly bristling with thorns, that tore our clothes and lacerated our hands and legs fearfully. All that day we trekked through a waterless section of the forest and suffered agonies from heat and thirst. Towards evening, however, we emerged on an open plain on the edge of a vast swamp. My two servants were advancing slightly ahead of me, and as they left the forest and saw the cold water ahead, they threw down their burdens and raced towards the marsh. At this instant I also broke from the entangling bushes on the edge of the swamp and all but followed their example, so parched was I, when I beheld a sight that for a moment, kept me spellbound. As the natives reached the water-edge, two huge black forms rose, and with a snort of rage made for the unfortunate men. In a moment I had recognized the animals for the powerful, fearless wild buffalo of the Chhota Nagpur plateau. Unslinging my rifle from my shoulder, I fired at the animal nearest to me, but in my haste aimed too low, so that the bullet, intended for the shoulder, penetrated the animal's knee. The buffalo went down with a crash and as I turned to fire at its mate, I realized with a thrill of horror, that I was too late. The second unfortunate Indian, in his haste to leave the water, had slipped on the marshy banks and lay floundering in the mire. In a moment the buffalo was on him, and with one mighty sweep of its huge horns, hurled his body through the air to land a mangled mass of bones and flesh some ten feet from the bank. At this moment it spotted me, and with a snort of rage, charged in my direction. I am afraid I let no sporting sentiments interfere with my shooting. Working the bolt of my rifle steadily from my shoulder—my rifle being of the magazine pattern—put four successive shots into the huge brute in as many seconds, so that it went down as if pollaxed.

By this time my remaining servant, trembling with the shock of his recent experience, had reached my side, and reloading, I went towards the wounded buffalo. Although handicapped with its broken legs, the animal was nevertheless making a gallant effort to get out of the deep mire that hampered its movements. As we approached the beast, it glared at us, and with a savage bellow attempted to charge. Awaiting till it had approached sufficiently close, one well-directed shot put an end to its miseries, and we were safe to attend to our unfortunate comrade.

Poor fellow, he must have been killed instantaneously; covering up the body with a piece of cloth, we dug a shallow grave and buried him as decently as possible. By this time it was getting dark, so we built a fire and camped a short distance away.

That night I slept badly. The excitement of the evening and the strangeness of the situation kept me continuously awake. Towards morning the cold became intense, and unable to sleep, I determined to rise, replenish the fire and if possible boil some water for an early cup of tea.

Leaving the shelter of the bush in which I lay, I walked briskly towards the place where I had seen Mohamed Ali stock our small store of edibles. Unable to find them, I was first under the impression that I had mistaken the spot, but a closer inspection showed a few remaining packages containing flour and sugar. Shouting loudly to Mohamed Ali to wake up, I started a feverish search in the surrounding bushes for further signs of the stores, but although I wandered far into the forest, not a single trace of food could I find. Incensed with Mohamed Ali for his carelessness and blaming myself bitterly for not carefully attending to the storing of this essential part of our equipment more carefully, I awaited the arrival of my servant impatiently, determined to give him a bit of my mind.

I must have waited fully half an hour, still searching round in the hope of finding part of the missing stores, before I was aware that no Mohamed Ali had turned up.

'What on earth is the matter with the fellow,' I wondered. 'He surely cannot be still asleep.'

Returning to the camp, I looked all round for him. His blanket lay in a ruffled heap on the spot where he had slept, but of the man himself there was no trace.

All that morning I waited, searching the surrounding forest and even firing my rifle occasionally in the hope of attracting his attention if the poor fellow had wandered into the forest and lost his direction, but to no avail, and at last I was compelled to admit that henceforth I would have to travel alone.

Imagine my position. One of my servants killed, two mysteriously spirited away in the dead of night, and no provision of any sort except a little flour and sugar to sustain me till I reached a human habitation of some type.

To say I was depressed, is to put it mildly. Candidly, I was more than depressed, I was scared. The vision of myself parched with thirst, faint from starvation, wandering through the dense forest, a prey to any wild animal I chanced to meet, filled me with the gravest apprehensions.

Keep on, I knew I had to. To stay where I was, would only diminish my chances of reaching civilization, so that, while I had the strength and ability, I determined to push on depending on my good fortune to strike some village.

Cutting first a generous supply of meat from the carcass of one of the buffaloes I had shot the evening previous, I packed the few things I needed and, with as much ammunition as I could carry, set out on my lonely trek.

All that day I worked steadily south-east, but although I kept a sharp lookout, I failed to detect any signs of human habitation. That night, fearing to sleep on the ground alone, I looked around for a convenient tree, and after singeing a portion of the meat over a small fire, I ate a frugal meal, and climbed to the topmost branches.

The evening was still light and I scanned the forest in every direction. On every side was an unending vista of green and yellow leaves broken here and there by small clearings, but of villages no sign existed.

The night fell quickly, and soon a glorious moon sailed over the tree tops flooding the rustling, billowy sea of green below me, with a soft translucent light. It was a night, which in spite of my precarious position, I recall with the keenest delight.

Scarcely had the darkness fallen when a sambur belled in a thicket nearby and soon the forest awoke to its nocturnal life of mystery and movement.

From my lofty perch, I watched a herd of spotted deer troop past my tree, pursued by a stealthy yellow form which I instantly recognized for a huge leopard. I could have shot the beast easily, so unaware was he of any human presence, but I refrained from firing and later was thankful for this forbearance.

As the night wore on, I settled myself more comfortably in the deep fork of the tree and was soon asleep.

I may have slept a couple of hours, perhaps less, when I was awakened by a peculiar throbbing sound that seemed to fill the forest.

I roused myself, and looking round eagerly, soon detected the direction from which the sound was proceeding. As it approached, I recognized the low droaning of the large drums the Sontals in this district use and I must confess the thought of human beings filled me with a strange sensation of joy and relief.

Fortunately a natural prudence restrained me from springing from my perch and hastening in the direction of the drums. Waiting till the first of the drummers emerged from the thick forest, I raised myself and was about to call out, when I noticed that the leading natives, bearing huge flaming torches, were nude, except for a single loincloth and grotesquely decorated in yellow and vermillion. The torch-bearers were followed by others hideously painted in white and black representing skeletons. These extraordinary beings were executing a wired type of dance and chanting a solemn dirge, while immediately behind them, slung from bamboo poles, were the bodies of two men. The vanguard of this strange procession was formed of a large crowd of Sontals armed with spears, bows and arrows, and various other crude weapons.

The procession passed immediately under my tree, and as the bearers of the two corpses (as I took them to be) were beneath me, I looked down and received quite a shock—the bodies were those of our guide and my servant Mohamed Ali.

Waiting till the procession had passed, I took my rifle, and slipping from the tree, followed cautiously in their wake. I had not far to go. Reaching a clearing, the procession stopped. As the dancers and musicians advanced, each threw his burning torch on the ground and in a little while there were a heap of torches burning fiercely, around which the whole procession gathered.

Concealing myself in the bushes, a short distance out of the circle of light, I watched in amazement the strange rites that now followed.

First of all, the two bodies were laid side by side on the ground close to the fire. Two of the dancers—more grotesquely decorated than the others and whom I rightly conjectured were high priests of this strange sect—advanced and raising each body in turn, set the pole into a hollow in the ground, so that the bodies now confronted the dancers in an upright position. The instant the firelight fell on their faces, I realized with a thrill of horror that both men were alive, but so drugged or otherwise stupefied that they hung loosely in their fastenings, swaying like drunken beings.

No sooner was this done, than the whole circle of dancers sprang into activity. Round and round the fire they whirled, chanting a queer plaintive refrain, punctuated with staccato beats from the muffled drums. For a long while they danced till, at last weary with their exertions, they gave a final shout and settled down once more.

The two priests now advanced. Going up to the captives they

raised their heads and forced them to drink some concoction which they poured from a pitcher brought by one of the dancers. Whatever the drink was, it must have been a powerful restorative. Within five minutes both men were fully awake and conscious of all that was taking place round them.

What, I wondered, would be the ultimate fate of these two men. It was not likely that in a district so near to British administration they would attempt a cold-blooded murder, but had I known what was to follow, death would have been a merciful release.

Seeing that both men were now perfectly conscious, one of the priests arose and taking a long sharp knife in his hands advanced towards his victims. I fingered my trigger uneasily, uncertain to fire or not, but determined at all cost to save the lives of those two servants of mine. Instead of injuring them, however, he commenced a long harangue. Pointing frequently towards the prisoners and then into the forest in the direction in which I had come, he seemed to be working his followers up to some momentous decision and he was not long in gaining their unanimous support. The moment he stopped, with one voice, the whole tribe chanted 'Maro, maro' (Kill, kill) and, with a swiftness that completely deceived me, the priest struck twice, and the red blood gushed down the chests of the victims. Quickly I slung my rifle round, bringing the foresight to bear on the murderer. But from the moment of that one fierce shout and the anguished cry from the two prisoners, not a further sound could be heard. A strange tense expectant hush seemed to fill the forest. On the face of the two prisoners were depicted the most abject terror, their wounds, probably superficial, bled profusely, but the men were unaware of the blood, instead they stood staring before them into the forest, waiting for some awful apparition to come, and come it did.

Swiftly, silently, remorseless as death itself came a queer sinister shape. Not two feet high, semi-human in form, its hair, straggling and entangled all over its body, its face hideous, with two great eyes darting out of cavernous sockets, it leapt and gambolled out of the forest, into the clearing, and with a shrill maniacal laugh, stood confronting the two prisoners.

So hideous, so repulsive was this awful creature, that my rifle forgotten, I stood staring, unable to believe my eyes; and then started a dance the likes of which I have never seen.

Whirling slowly at first, advancing, retreating, this grotesque human shape, fluttered up and down before the terror-stricken silent men. Gradually the pace increased, a drum commenced to throb gently, swifter grew the dance and louder grew the drums and louder the chanting of the priests joined the roll of the drums; slowly, one by one, the other dancers joined in, the spectators swayed by a common impulse beat time to the ever swelling music, and the prisoners, hypnotized by the rhythm of sound and movement round them, sank lower and lower, till they hung inert, their bonds alone supporting them.

The end came suddenly, dramatically. A rifle shot rang out a sharp command, and a thin line of khaki-clad figures broke from the cover of the jungle and surrounded the dancers.

In a moment pandemonium broke loose. Surprised, startled and wholly unprepared, the dancers and priests broke and fled for the cover of the surrounding forests. Anxious to join the melee, I broke from the cover of the forest and rushed towards the fire. At that instant, I came face to face with one of the presiding priest.

With a fine disregard for sacerdotal procedure, I jammed my rifle butt into his ribs that he went down with a groan and stayed there. Reaching my two servants, I hastened to undo their bonds, and while engaged in this task, I was suddenly seized from behind and swinging round found myself face to face with a young Police Officer.

'Well I'm damned. If it isn't the very man we are looking for,' he cried with surprise. 'What on earth are you doing here?'

'Can't you see,' I said, 'Getting these two poor devils out of the scrape they have got into.'

Mutual explanation followed and I learned that from the moment I had left Daltonganj I had been shadowed by members of this tribe under the mistaken impression that I was an Excise Officer on one of my periodical raids into the interior. The guide had been overpowered and carried off the first night in the hope that without a guide further progress would be impossible, but as I continued, all unknown to me, in the right direction, my servant Mohamed Ali suffered the same fate.

Anxious to avenge themselves on what they considered were informers of the Police, these two men were taken into the heart of the forest and handed over to the 'Soul Catchers'. The rites I witnessed were explained to me by the young Police Officer who had arrived on the scene so opportunely.

The men were first drugged with a native concoction containing bhang. On arrival at the scene of operations, they were given an antidote and restorative, and later branded in the chest by the priests, so that they were marked men for life. Next a strange half-demented creature, who lived in that part of the forest and who was credited with supernatural powers, danced before the victims who were thus hypnotized and in this condition made to believe that their souls had left them and were in the keeping of the 'Soul Catchers'. They were seldom harmed physically, but were socially ostracized, driven from village to village and refused even the ordinary necessities of life. The hardships of such an existence usually drove these poor creatures crazy or they died from starvation and neglect. None dared to assist them for fear of incurring the enmity of the 'Soul Catchers' themselves. There was, however, a method of release and many took this course. By selling all they possessed, they would raise the necessary amount of money needed, and this on being paid to the high priest of the sect, a ceremony was performed by which the unfortunate victim regained his soul and his position in society. Although in the turmoil that followed the first rush of the Police, the strange creature I had seen eluded the troops and disappeared in the forest, the high priest of the sect I had knocked senseless with my rifle was secured and duly appeared in court. I will never forget the sensation he created, when in his full regalia, he appeared in the dock to answer the charges against him. Although I formed the principal witness, he produced an alibi that was unshakable. In fact the whole village turned out en masse, prepared to swear that on that particular night this same priest was asleep in his self but in the middle of the village—and that—the whole case was a police plot brought up out of spite.

He was eventually convicted and got three years hard, and the tribe of 'Soul Catchers' shifted to healthier quarters, but to this day I never visit Daltonganj and the neighbouring villages without a strange sensation of being watched and spied on.

PENDLEBURY'S TROPHY

John Eyton

I

Arthur St John Pendlebury—known to his intimates as 'Pen'—was the beau-ideal of the cavalry subaltern, with plenty of friends, money and self-assurance. Before he had been in the country a year, India was at his feet; this is not to say that he had overstudied her languages or customs, but that he had sufficient means for fulfilling any of his aspirations, which were limited to picnics, polo ponies and shikar trophies. To the latter his first long leave was devoted. To one who has stalked the Highland stag under the eye of an experienced man, the stag of Kashmir seems easy game, and satisfaction was in Pendlebury's eye as he ran it over his pile of kit on Rawalpindi station: new portmanteau; new gun-cases, containing his twelve-bore, his Mannlicher Schonhauer, his Holland and Holland High Velocity; fieldglasses and telescope; kodak, for recording triumphs; new tent, fully equipped with every device for comfort and cooking altogether a capital outfit, pointing to an interesting addition to the Scotch heads in the hall at Pendlebury, for he could not fail to bag a Kashmiri stag or two in three weeks. To this sentiment Ali Baksh, his Mohammedan servant, agreed in perfect English…

capital man, Ali Baksh—a real treasure.

The drive from Rawalpindi to Srinagar was quite pleasant, the scenery being almost English, though the road was only soso. On arrival, Pendlebury resisted the tame temptations of picnic-making, and got down to business at once. He was not going to be bothered with consulting the old local bores in the Club, because the obvious thing to do was to get hold of a native fellow who could talk English a bit, and knew the ropes from A to Z, and such a man was known to Ali Baksh, who would find him out quietly and persuade him to accompany the saheb. His friend, he said, was the best man in Kashmir, who being in constant request, would accompany only noted shikaris. Ali Baksh tactfully insinuated that Pendlebury belonged to the latter category, and Pendlebury of course believed him—for even the finished product of Eton and the Bullingdon is often singularly artless in the experienced hands of an Indian bearer.

At eleven o'clock on the morning after arrival, Ali Baksh produced the paragon, whose name was also something Baksh Pir, Baksh, Pendlebury believed him to say. He was a fine-looking, well-set-up fellow, with fierce moustaches and glittering eyes; nicely turned out too, with a khaki suit of military cut, mauve shirt and neat puttees; he carried a long mountaineering pole, and had glasses slung in a leather case over his shoulder, and was altogether the type of what a shikari ought to look, and indeed does look in magazine illustrations. To the experienced old bores in the Club, he might have appeared to overdo the part, but to Pendlebury he was the very thing. Besides, he knew all the likely spots, had excellent chits from officers in quite good regiments, indicating invariable success, and, lastly, got on well with Ali Baksh.

So Pir Baksh was engaged on the spot—for the modest sum

of one hundred rupees, paid in advance, for the three weeks' trip, and on the understanding that he would waste no time over uncertainties, but would lead on direct to the spot where an astounding stag had been marked down. About this stag there was no doubt whatever, for Pir Baksh himself resided in its neighbourhood, and knew its haunts and habits so well that the stag might almost be said to be one of the family. He had been keeping it, he said, for a General, but could not resist the temptation of seeing it fall to the rifle of so noble a saheb as Pendlebury. They parted quite effusively, after payment had been made, and Ali Baksh accompanied Pir Baksh to make the bandobast. Pendlebury washed his hands of these matters, so naturally did not see Pir hand over the stipulated thirty rupees to his friend Ali outside.

As Pendlebury remarked in the mess on his return from leave. 'What I like about this country is that you only have to get hold of a good servant, tell him what you want to do and how you like it, and say "Bazar chalo, bandobast kayo." He'll do the rest. Now I had a first-class bandobast up in Kashmir—never had to say a word myself; no use messing a good man about.'

And so it was—his two men certainly were not messed about, for between them they did everything, and ran Pendlebury— engaging ponies and carriers on the basis of a twenty per cent commission for themselves; leading in men from the shops, who staggered beneath a vast weight of stores, some of which were destined for Pendlebury's consumption; making a great show of polishing things and cleaning clean rifles. There was nothing wrong with that bandobast, and Pendlebury could well afford to pay the hundred and fifty odd rupees, which it was found necessary to disburse. In fact, the charm of the whole thing was that Pendlebury believed throughout that he was saving money—a fact which redounds to the credit of the astute pair.

The start for the first camp was worth watching; first rode Pendlebury, every inch a cavalry officer, his blue eyes full of good humour, and his cheeks quite pink with excitement; his shooting suit was good to look upon, and Ali Baksh could certainly polish boots. At a respectful distance behind him rode Pir Baksh, resplendent in Jodhpur breeches, while, last of all, Ali marshalled the kit, a fine staff in one hand, and in the other that emblem of the bearer, a brass hurricane lamp. It was a procession to be proud of, and successful shikar was in the very air.

The haunt of the famous stage was ten marches away, and Pendlebury beguiled them with small-game shooting and the taking of snapshots. The marches were very well run, and it was not the fault of Pir Baksh that the leather suitcase, the telescope, and the cartridge bag got lost in the process of crossing a river. In fact, Pendlebury thought Pir Baksh had behaved very openly about the whole thing, and had seemed to regard the matter as a personal loss—whereas, in truth, it was exactly the opposite. But for this mishap all went swimmingly.

They reached the little village at the edge of the forest in the evening, and Pendlebury's tent was pitched under delightful chenal trees near a little stream which looked first-class for trout. He could hardly sleep for excitement, and lay awake picturing the record stag and its record head, and hearing the sound of a high-pitched song in the bazaar, where, had he but known it, Pir and Ali were entertaining the local shikaris at his expense. Finally he shouted, '*Choop. Choop karo ek dam!*' and lay back with the satisfaction of one whose commands are obeyed.

Next day it was arranged that Pir Baksh should go for khabar of the stag, while Pendlebury fished the river for trout.

So Pendlebury sallied out with his split-cane and fly-boxes, and a man to carry his net, and another man to bear his lunch, while Pir Baksh, with his glasses and pole and preposterous jodhpuris, departed in the opposite direction. It was curious that so confident and so famous a shikari should require the assistance of a local man, a stranger of ragged and unkempt appearance—but we will suppose that he too needed some one to carry his lunch.

Pendlebury had a pleasant enough day by the bright, clear stream, and brought home several minute trout for his dinner. Of the movements of Pir Baksh little is known, except that he went quite a distance into the forest, starting at 10 a.m. and returning at noon, after which hour he sat with Ali and the local talent in the bazaar. Yet, when he was announced at 8 p.m., he entered the tent wearily enough, with much bazaar dust on his boots and puttees—so much that Pendlebury could see that the fellow had had a pretty stiff day of it. Pir Baksh was mysterious and confidential; in response to Pendlebury's eager inquiries, he allowed that he had seen the stag, but when Pendlebury whooped with delight, he qualified this intelligence with the remark that the stag was bahut hoshiar, and had only arrived on the scene in the late evening, after a complete day of tireless, lonely watching on the part of Pir Baksh. He had heard the stag at intervals and had not dared to move for fear of making it nervous. It would be as well to let it rest, under due observation, for a day or two, and then make certain of it. Incidentally he had heard in the bazaar on his return that another saheb, a well-known hunter, had set his heart on this stag and had hunted it for a month, but, since he had not seen fit to engage the services of Pir Baksh, he had not had a shot. It was finally suggested that Pendlebury would do well to visit a noted pool three miles down stream for the next day or two, and this Pendlebury agreed to do. After all, Pir Baksh knew the ropes, and this stag was worth waiting for.

So for the next two days Pendlebury lashed the stream for trout, while each morning Pir Baksh started with a set face for the jungle and spent the day in the bazaar, arriving each evening at a later hour and more visibly weary and dusty. Each evening, too, the antlers of the stag had grown with its cunning. Rowland Ward's book, which Pendlebury of course carried, had no record in it to touch this head, as described by Pir Baksh; to Rowland Ward the head should go for setting up—none of your local mochis. Pendlebury saw the footnote in that book, 'Shot by A. St J. Pendlebury, Esq, the Blue Hussars, Kashmir, 1920. A remarkable head, with record points, length and span'. On the third evening Pir Baksh was very late indeed. Pendlebury had turned in, and had long lain listening to a perfect orgy in the bazaar, when, about midnight, Ali Baksh gave that deprecating cough whereby the Indian servant makes known his humble presence, and announced Pir Baksh.

A tired, grimy, dusty picture he made in the light of the electric torch, and a pitiful tale he told. He had sat up without food for a day and half a night

'Bahut kaam kiya, saheb. Main bilkull bhuka ho gya—bilkull. Kuchh nahin khaya gya.'

Great indeed had been the sufferings of the worthy man (considering they had been experienced in the bazaar), but he had seen the stag at close quarters, and something told him that the saheb would shoot it tomorrow.

Such a stag—a Barasingha indeed, with antlers like trees, and it roar like a river; such a stag had not been seen for twenty years, when 'Ismith' saheb had missed just such a one, and had given him, Pir Baksh, his new rifle and a hundred golis, vowing he would never shoot again...'*Kabhi ham aisa barawala nahin dekha.*' Pendlebury was, of course, half out of his mind with excitement, and, had it been feasible, he would have gone out there and then and tried conclusions. As it was, he contented himself with lauding Pir Baksh to the skies, an honour which the latter accepted with sweet humility. He would make the bandobast; they would start out after tiffin, and would lie up till the evening. Let the saheb have no doubts; he would slay that stag, and his name would be great in Kashmir...'*Kuchh shaqq nahin hai; qaza zarur hoga...zarur.*'

Like an echo outside the tent, Ali Baksh repeated the comforting 'zarur'.

II

Pendlebury arose at 6 a.m. for the stag which he was to see at 6 p.m., and spent the most nerve-racking morning of his life. He cut himself shaving; he fiddled with his rifles, and asked a dozen times whether he should take the High Velocity or the little Mannlicher; he counted out ten rounds of ammunition and laid them ready...then decided to rake the other rifle, and counted out twenty more; then, finally changed his mind and decided to take both, with about thirty rounds; he stuffed his pipe too full, and broke the vulcanite stem in tapping it out; changed his boots three times; smoked quantities of cigarettes, and burnt a hole in his copy of Rowland Ward with one of them; and had neither a good breakfast nor a sufficient lunch.

In fact Pendlebury did his utmost to spoil his eye and his hand, instead of strolling out with a rod and forgetting the great stag in the excitement of landing a pound trout, as any of the old bores at the Club would have advised him to do.

At last the great moment arrived, and Ali Baksh whispered, 'Pir Baksh here, sir.' With an immense effort Pendlebury assumed the nonchalance he did not feel, and strolled out of the tent, where he found Pir Baksh carrying a rifle and looking very businesslike in ancient garments; a ragged, disreputable stranger had the other rifle. When Pendlebury, who was feeling nervous enough already, objected to the latter's presence, Pir Baksh pointed out the advantages of having a man on the spot to help skin the shikar, and so had his way. On the way Pendlebury did a great many things which the old bores at the Club would have deprecated: he smoked too many cigarettes—'to steady his nerves'; he slogged along instead of walking quietly, thus laying up a clammy shirt for himself in the evening; also, he cursed the men for not hurrying, and then cursed still more when, half-way, he discovered that he had forgotten his second-best pipe, his flask and his sandwiches. However, it was too late to do anything then.

They climbed uphill through thick forest bordering a little hill stream till they came to an open glen, with green moss at their feet and tall trees around them. Half-way up the glen Pir Baksh whispered a halt, and Pendlebury was led behind the trunk of a fallen tree, where he was asked to wait, without moving, while Pir Baksh and the stranger moved furtively off under cover of the trees.

Hours seemed to pass as Pendlebury fingered his Mannlicher, the final choice, expecting every moment to see the dark shape loom in the glen. Time and time again he opened his breech to see if the thing were working, and feverishly moved the backsight up and down the slide, finally leaving it at five hundred yards, when a sudden sound startled him.

It was booming, long-drawn...the unmistakable roar of a

stag far above him. He was at once certain that Pir Baksh had messed up the whole show, and that he ought to be farther up the glen; it would be dark for a certainty before the stag moved down; it was getting dark already. A twig cracked behind him, and he turned to see Pir Baksh behind him, holding his finger to his lips.

'*Barawala ata*,' whispered Pir Baksh, while Pendlebury got into a position of readiness; there was no doubt about the approach of the stag, for it roared more than once, and was evidently moving down the little stream.

A quarter of an hour passed—the sun sank—still no view of the stag; in five minutes it would be too dark to see the foresight. Pendlebury began to fidget, when suddenly Pir Baksh touched his arm, and pointed...a dark shape was moving under the trees by the stream.

'*Woh hai, saheb*,' whispered Pir Baksh. '*Maro. Maro. Zarur lag jaega.*'

Pendlebury aimed his wavering piece in the direction of the dark shape, and squeezed the trigger...

There was a flash and a kick—then a commotion under the trees, as a big animal splashed with a snort through the tiny stream and crashed into the undergrowth beyond—farther and farther away.

'Damn!' said Pendlebury—not so Pir Baksh, who sprang to his feet with a wild, '*Lag gya. Lag gya. Zakhmi hai*,' and, motioning to Pendlebury to stay where he was, ran towards the stream, throwing out a parting, '*Milega zarur.*'

It was quite dark when Pir Baksh returned and informed the ecstatic Pendlebury that the stag '*sekht zakhmi ho gya. Khun bahut hai. Aiye, saheb.*' Up jumped Pendlebury and followed across the glen and the stream, where Pir Baksh borrowed his electric torch and searched the ground...yes, there was blood...first a mere drop on a leaf; then, five yards on, a bigger splash; farther still, a regular patch dyeing the ground. Pir Baksh explained that the beast had been hit forward—a truly wonderful shot—and had carried on to die. He would be found quite dead in the morning—till then there was nothing to be done.

On the way home, Pir Baksh, in the intervals of exultation, promised to make an early start, dissuading Pendlebury from accompanying him by remarking that this was only poor shikari's work, unsuitable for the Saheb Bahadur. Pendlebury was fagged out, and let him have his way; before he went to bed, he had a last loving look at the Mannlicher, which he found sighted at five hundred yards! This he put down to carelessness in carrying, and congratulated himself that he had not had it at five hundred when he fired; good shot as it had been, he would not have put the beast at over seventy yards...funny how he had felt certain that he had hit him before Pir Baksh spoke!

III

Pendlebury's next morning was almost as bad as the last. He clung to the camp, springing out of his chair at the slightest sound; he had occasion to throw his boots at Ali because the latter had made a noise like Pir; once more he failed to do justice to his meals, and spent the day alternating between triumph and despair. But the hours never brought Pir Baksh, and at last he turned into bed and lay awake, listening. Presently he heard a hubbub, then saw lights outside. As he sprang out of bed he was greeted with the welcome, '*Mil gya...saheb,*' in the dulcet tones of Pir Baksh; he rushed out, and there, amid a crowd of admiring servants, stood Pir Baksh himself, grimed with mud and dust from head to foot, his clothes artistically torn, blood on his coat but in his hands great antlers, branching out from a draggled mask.

Pendlebury whooped; the servants sucked in their breath with wonder; and Pir Baksh, in shrill tones, raised his paean of victory. Twenty miles had he toiled; fifteen hours without food; but for the saheb's honour he would have dropped with fatigue and died. Even in death the great stag had been wondrous cunning, and would never have been brought to book but for the superior cunning of Pir Baksh; there had been a personal encounter, in which danger had been gladly braved for the saheb, and a valuable life risked. Great was the name of 'Pendlebury saheb', who gives life to poor men, even to the humble shikari, beneath his feet…

This stirring recital—composed that day in the bazaar—was followed by that little lull which tactfully indicates baksheesh to the least imaginative of us, and Pendlebury rose to the occasion nobly. There was a hundred-rupee note for Pir Baksh; twenty for the disreputable stranger who had given *bahri madad*, and who was described as a '*sidha admi…kam kerne wala bhi*'; twenty more for Ali Baksh for being a good fellow; and mithai for all the camp. Pendlebury did things handsomely.

◆

The old Club bores might, with reason, have sniffed at that head had they seen it; but, as it happens, it was packed straight off to Pendlebury's agents in Bombay, for shipping to London, on the advice of Pir Baksh—so there was no one to call attention to a resemblance between these antlers and a pair produced by the disreputable stranger aforesaid on the occasion of Pir Baksh's first visit to the bazaar. In point of fact, both pairs had a similar chip off of one of the brow points.

The stranger had asked twenty rupees for this pair...but who can fathom the mind of the East?

Another trivial detail...Pir Baksh and the said stranger had slain a young stag on the second day; while Pendlebury was fishing, for they had feasted the village with fresh venison that night. It was also on record that Pir Baksh had retained the mask, and had bottled a small quantity of blood.

One more fact—Pendlebury had been mistaken about his sighting, and the stag at which he fired in the dusk was not a warrantable one; at least, so the stranger informed me afterwards. Not that it matters, for the shot went well over its back.

But what matters? The great head has the pride of place at Pendlebury Hall, and Pendlebury is happy whenever he sees it.

And, anyway, Pir Baksh was an artist.

THE EYE OF THE EAGLE

Ruskin Bond

It was a high, piercing sound, almost like the yelping of a dog. Jai stopped picking the wild strawberries that grew in the grass around him, and looked up at the sky. He had a dog—a shaggy guard-dog called Motu—but Motu did not yet yelp, he growled and barked. The strange sound came from the sky, and Jai had heard it before. Now, realizing what it was, he jumped to his feet, calling to his dog, calling his sheep to start for home. Motu came bounding towards him, ready for a game.

'Not now, Motu,' said Jai. 'We must get the lambs home quickly.' Again he looked up at the sky.

He saw it now, a black speck against the sun, growing larger as it circled the mountain, coming lower every moment—a Golden Eagle, king of the skies over the higher Himalayas, ready now to swoop and seize its prey.

Had it seen a pheasant or a pine marten? Or was it after one of the lambs? Jai had never lost a lamb to an eagle, but recently some of the other shepherds had been talking about a golden eagle that had been preying on their flocks.

The sheep had wandered some way down the side of the mountain, and Jai ran after them to make sure that none of the lambs had gone off on its own.

Motu ran about, barking furiously. He wasn't very good at keeping the sheep together—he was often bumping into them and sending them tumbling down the slope—but his size and bear—like look kept the leopards and wolves at a distance.

Jai was counting the lambs; they were bleating loudly and staying close to their mothers. *One—two—three—four...*

There should have been a fifth. Jai couldn't see it on the slope below him. He looked up towards a rocky ledge near the steep path to the Tung temple. The golden eagle was circling the rocks.

The bird disappeared from sight for a moment, then rose again with a small creature grasped firmly in its terrible talons.

'It has taken a lamb!' shouted Jai. He started scrambling up the slope. Motu ran ahead of him, barking furiously at the big bird as it glided away over the tops of the stunted junipers to its eyrie on the cliffs above Tung.

There was nothing that Jai and Motu could do except stare helplessly and angrily at the disappearing eagle. The lamb had died the instant it had been struck. The rest of the flock seemed unaware of what had happened. They still grazed on the thick, sweet grass of the mountain slopes.

'We had better drive them home, Motu,' said Jai, and at a nod from the boy, the big dog bounded down the slope, to take part in his favourite game of driving the sheep homewards. Soon he had them running all over the place, and Jai had to dash about trying to keep them together. Finally they straggled homewards.

'A fine lamb gone,' said Iai to himself gloomily. 'I wonder what Grandfather will say.'

Grandfather said, 'Never mind. It had to happen some day. That eagle has been watching the sheep for some time.'

Grandmother, more practical, said; 'We could have sold the lamb for three hundred rupees. You'll have to be more careful in future, Jai. Don't fall asleep on the hillside, and don't read story books when you are supposed to be watching the sheep!'

'I wasn't reading this morning,' said Jai truthfully, forgetting to mention that he had been gathering strawberries.

'It's good for him to read,' said Grandfather, who had never had the luck to go to school. In his days, there weren't any schools in the mountains. Now there was one in every village.

'Time enough to read at night,' said Grandmother, who did not think much of the little one-room school down at Maku, their home village.

'Well, these are the October holidays,' said Grandfather. 'Otherwise he would not be here to help us with the sheep. It will snow by the end of the month, and then we will move with the flock. You will have more time for reading then, Jai.'

At Maku, which was down in the warmer valley, Jai's parents tilled a few narrow terraces on which they grew barley, millets and potatoes. The old people brought their sheep up to the Tung meadows to graze during the summer months. They stayed in a small stone hut just off the path which pilgrims took to the ancient temple. At 12,000 feet above sea level, it was the highest Hindu temple on the inner Himalayan ranges.

The following day Jai and Motu were very careful. The did not let the sheep out of sight even for a minute. Nor did they catch sight of the golden eagle. 'What if it attacks again?' wondered Jai. 'How will I stop it?'

The great eagle, with its powerful beak and talons, was more than a match for boy or dog. Its hind claw, four inches round the curve, was its most dangerous weapon. When it spread its wings, the distance from tip to tip was more than eight feet.

The eagle did not come that day because it had fed well and was now resting in its eyrie. Old bones, which had belonged to pheasants, snow-cocks, pine martens and even foxes, were scattered about the rocks which formed the eagle's home. The eagle had a mate, but it was not the breeding season and she was away on a scouting expedition of her own.

The golden eagle stood on its rocky ledge, staring majestically across the valley. Its hard, unblinking eyes missed nothing. Those strange orange-yellow eyes could spot a field—rat or a mouse-hare more than a hundred yards below.

There were other eagles on the mountain, but usually they kept to their own territory. And only the bolder ones went for lambs, because the flocks were always protected by men and dogs.

The eagle took off from its eyrie and glided gracefully, powerfully over the valley, circling the Tung mountain.

Below lay the old temple, built from slabs of grey granite. A line of pilgrims snaked up the steep, narrow path. On the meadows below the peak, the sheep grazed peacefully, unaware of the presence of the eagle. The great bird's shadow slid over the sunlit slopes.

The eagle saw the boy and the dog, but he did not fear them. He had his eye on a lamb that was frisking about on the grass, a few feet away from the other grazing sheep.

Jai did not see the eagle until it swept round an outcrop of rocks about a hundred feet away. It moved silently, without any movement of its wings, for it had already built up the momentum for its dive. Now it came straight at the lamb.

Motu saw the bird in time. With a low growl he dashed forward and reached the side of the lamb at almost the same instant that the eagle swept in.

There was a terrific collision. Feathers flew. The eagle screamed with rage. The lamb tumbled down the slope, and Motu howled in pain as the huge beak struck him high on the leg.

The big bird, a little stunned by the clash, flew off rather unsteadily, with a mighty beating of its wings.

Motu had saved the lamb. It was frightened but unhurt. Bleating loudly, it joined the other sheep, who took up the bleating. Jai ran up to Motu, who lay whimpering on the ground. There was no sign of the eagle. Quickly he removed his shirt and vest; then he wrapped his vest round the dog's wound, tying it in position with his belt.

Motu could not get up, and he was much too heavy for Jai to carry. Jai did not want to leave his dog alone, in case the eagle returned to attack.

He stood up, cupped his hand to his mouth, and began calling for his grandfather.

'Dada, dada!' he shouted, and presently Grandfather heard him and came stumbling down the slope. He was followed by another shepherd, and together they lifted Motu and carried him home.

Motu had a bad wound, but Grandmother cleaned it and applied a paste made of herbs. Then she laid strips of carrot over the wound—an old mountain remedy—and bandaged the leg. But it would be some time before Motu could run about again. By then it would probably be snowing and time to leave these high—altitude pastures and return to the valley. Meanwhile, the sheep had to be taken out to graze, and Grandfather decided to accompany Jai for the remaining period.

They did not see the golden eagle for two or three days, and, when they did, it was flying over the next range. Perhaps it had found some other source of food, or even another flock of sheep. 'Are you afraid of the eagle?' Grandfather asked Jai.

'I wasn't before,' said Jai. 'Not until it hurt Motu. I did not know it could be so dangerous. But Motu hurt it too. He banged straight into it!'

'Perhaps it won't bother us again,' said Grandfather thoughtfully. 'A bird's wing is easily injured—even an eagle's.'

Jai wasn't so sure. He had seen it strike twice, and he knew that it was not afraid of anyone. Only when it learnt to fear his presence would it keep away from the flock.

The next day Grandfather did not feel well; he was feverish and kept to his bed. Motu was hobbling about gamely on three legs; the wounded leg was still very sore.

'Don't go too far with the sheep,' said Grandmother. 'Let them graze near the house.'

'But there's hardly any grass here,' said Jai.

'I don't want you wandering off while that eagle is still around.'

'Give him my stick,' said Grandfather from his bed. Grandmother took it from the corner and handed it to the boy.

It was an old stick, made of wild cherry wood, which Grandfather often carried around. The wood was strong and well-seasoned; the stick was stout and long. It reached upto Jai's shoulders.

'Don't lose it,' said Grandfather. 'It was given to me many years ago by a wandering scholar who came to the Tung temple. I was going to give it to you when you got bigger, but perhaps this is the right time for you to have it. If the eagle comes near you, swing the stick around your head. That should frighten it off!'

Clouds had gathered over the mountains, and a heavy mist hid the Tung temple. With the approach of winter, the flow of pilgrims had been reduced to a trickle. The shepherds had started leaving the lush meadows and returning to their villages at lower altitudes. Very soon the bears and the leopards and the golden eagles would have the high ranges all to themselves.

Jai used the cherry wood stick to prod the sheep along the path until they reached the steep meadows. The stick would have to be a substitute for Motu. And they seemed to respond to it more readily than they did to Motu's mad charges.

Because of the sudden cold and the prospect of snow, Grandmother had made Jai wear a rough woollen jacket and a pair of high boots bought from a Tibetan trader. He wasn't used to the boots—he wore sandals at other times—and had some difficulty in climbing quickly up and down the hillside. It was tiring work, trying to keep the flock together. The cawing of some crows warned Jai that the eagle might be around, but the mist prevented him from seeing very far.

After some time the mist lifted and Jai was able to see the temple and the snow-peaks towering behind it. He saw the golden eagle, too. It was circling high overhead. Jai kept close to the flock—one eye on the eagle, one eye on the restless sheep.

Then the great bird stooped and flew lower. It circled the temple and then pretended to go away. Jai felt sure it would be back. And a few minutes later it reappeared from the other side of the mountain. It was much lower now, wings spread out and back, taloned feet to the fore, piercing eyes fixed on its target—a small lamb that had suddenly gone frisking down the slope, away from Jai and the flock.

Now it flew lower still, only a few feet off the ground, paying no attention to the boy.

It passed Jai with a great rush of air, and as it did so the boy struck out with his stick and caught the bird a glancing blow.

The eagle missed its prey, and the tiny lamb skipped away.

To Jai's amazement, the bird did not fly off. Instead it landed on the hillside and glared at the boy, as a king would glare at a humble subject who had dared to pelt him with a pebble.

The golden eagle stood almost as tall as Jai. Its wings were still outspread. Its fierce eyes seemed to be looking through and through the boy.

Jai's first instinct was to turn and run. But the cherry wood stick was still in his hands, and he felt sure there was power in it. He saw that the eagle was about to launch itself again at the lamb. Instead of running away, he ran forward, the stick raised above his head.

The eagle rose a few feet off the ground and struck out with its huge claws.

Luckily for Jai, his heavy jacket took the force of the blow. A talon ripped through the sleeve, and the sleeve fell away. At the same time the heavy stick caught the eagle across its open wing. The bird gave a shrill cry of pain and fury. Then it turned and flapped heavily away, flying unsteadily because of its injured wing.

Jai still clutched the stick, because he expected the bird to return; he did not even glance at his torn jacket. But the golden eagle had alighted on a distant rock and was in no hurry to return to the attack.

Jai began driving the sheep home. The clouds had become heavy and black, and presently the first snow flakes began to fall.

Jai saw a hare go lolloping done the hill. When it was about fifty yards away, there was a rush of air from the eagle's beating wings, and Jai saw the bird approaching the hare in a sidelong drive.

'So it hasn't been badly hurt,' thought Jai, feeling a little relieved, for he could not help admiring the great bird. 'Now it has found something else to chase for its dinner.'

The hare saw the eagle and dodged about, making for a clump of junipers. Jai did not know if it was caught or not, because the snow and sleet had increased and both bird and hare were lost in the gathering snow storm.

The sheep were bleating behind him. One of the lambs looked tired, and he stooped to pick it up. As he did so, he heard a thin, whining sound. It grew louder by the second. Before he could look up, a huge wing caught him across the shoulders and sent him sprawling. The lamb tumbled down the slope with him, into a thorny bilberry bush.

The bush saved them. Jai saw the eagle coming in again, flying low. It was another eagle! One had been vanquished, and now here was another, just as big and fearless, probably the mate of the first eagle.

Jai had lost his stick and there was no way in which he could fight the second eagle. So he crept further into the bush, holding the lamb beneath him. At the same time he began shouting at the top of his voice—both to scare the bird away and to summon help. The eagle could not easily get at them now; but the rest of the flock was exposed on the hillside. Surely the eagle would make for them.

Even as the bird circled and came back in another dive, Jai heard fierce barking. The eagle immediately swung away and rose skywards.

The barking came from Motu. Hearing Jai's shouts and sensing that something was wrong, he had come limping out of the house, ready to battle. Behind him came another shepherd and—most wonderful of all—Grandmother herself, banging two frying-pans together. The barking, the banging and the shouting frightened the eagles away. The sheep scattered too, and it was some time before they could all be rounded up. By then it was snowing heavily.

'Tomorrow we must all go down to Maku,' said the shepherd.

'Yes, it's time we went,' said Grandmother. 'You can read your story books again, Jai.'

'I'll have my own story to tell,' said Jai.

When they reached the hut and Jai saw Grandfather, he said, 'Oh, I've forgotten your stick!'

But Motu had picked it up. Carrying it between his teeth, he brought it home and sat down with it in the open doorway. He had decided the cherry wood was good for his teeth and would have chewed it up if Grandmother hadn't taken it from him.

'Never mind,' said Grandfather, sitting up on his cot. 'It isn't the stick that matters. It's the person who holds it.'

MUSTELA OF THE LONE HAND

C.G.D. Roberts

It was in the very heart of the ancient wood, the forest primeval of the North, gloomy with the dark-green crowded ranks of fir and spruce and hemlock, and tangled with the huge windfalls of countless storm-torn winters. But now, at high noon of the glowing Northern summer, the gloom was pierced to its depths with shafts of radiant sun; the barred and chequered transparent brown shadows hummed with dancing flies; the warm air was alive with the small, thin notes of chickadee and nuthatch, varied now and then by the impertinent scolding of the Canada jay; and the drowsing tree-tops steamed up an incense of balsamy fragrance in the heat. The ancient wilderness dreamed, stretched itself all open to the sun and seemed to sigh with immeasurable content.

High up in the grey trunk of a half-dead forest-giant was a round hole, the entrance to which had been the nest of a pair of big, red-headed, golden-winged woodpeckers, or 'yellow-hammers'. The big woodpeckers had long since been dispossessed—the female, probably, caught and devoured, with her eggs, upon the nest. The dispossesssor, and present tenant, was Mustela.

Framed in the blackness of the round hole was a sharp,

muzzled, triangular, golden-brown face with high, pointed ears, looking out upon the world below with keen eyes in which a savage wildness and an alert curiosity were incongruously mingled. Nothing that went on upon the dim ground far below, among the tangled trunks and windfalls, or in the sun-drenched tree-tops escaped that restless and piercing gaze. But Mustela had fed well, and felt lazy, and this hour of noon was not his hunting hour; so the most unsuspecting red squirrel, gathering cones in a neighbouring pine, was insufficient to lure him from his rest, and the plumpest hare, waving its long, suspicious ears down among the ground shadows, only made him lick his thin lips and think what he would do later on in the afternoon, when he felt like it.

Presently, however, a figure came into view at sight of which Mustela's expression changed. His thin black lips wrinkled back in a soundless snarl, displaying the full length of his long, snow-white, deadly-sharp canines, and a red spark of hate smouldered in his bright eyes. But no less than his hate was his curiosity—a curiosity which is the most dangerous weakness of all Mustela's tribe. Mustela's pointed head stretched itself clear of the hole, in order to get a better look at the man who was passing below his tree.

A man was a rare sight in that remote and inaccessible section of the Northern wilderness. This particular man—a woodsman, a 'timber-cruiser', seeking out new and profitable areas for the work of the lumbermen—wore a flaming red-and-orange handkerchief loosely knotted about his brawny neck, and carried over his shoulder an axe whose bright blade flashed sharply whenever a ray of sunlight struck it. It was this flashing axe and the blazing colour of the scarlet-and-orange kerchief that excited Mustela's curiosity—so excited it, indeed, that he came clean out of the hole and circled the great trunk, clinging close and wide-legged like a squirrel, in order to keep the woodsman in view as he passed by.

Engrossed though he was in the interesting figure of the man, Mustela's vigilance was still unsleeping. His amazingly quick ears at this moment caught a hushed hissing of wings in the air above his head. He did not stop to look up and investigate. Like a streak of ruddy light he flashed around the trunk and whisked back into his hole, and just as he vanished a magnificent long-winged goshawk, the king of all the falcons, swooping down from the blue, struck savagely with his clutching talons at the edges of the hole.

The quickness of Mustela was miraculous. Moreover, he was not content with escape. He wanted vengeance. Even in his lightning dive into his refuge he had managed to turn about, doubling on himself like an eel. And now, as those terrible talons gripped and clung for half a second to the edge of the hole, he snapped his teeth securely into the last joint of the longest talon and dragged it an inch or two in.

With a yelp of fury and surprise, the great falcon strove to lift himself into the air, pounding madly with his splendid wings and twisting himself about, and thrusting mightily with his free foot against the side of the hole. But he found himself held fast, as in a trap. Sagging back with all his weight, Mustela braced himself securely with all four feet and hung on, his whipcord sinews set like steel. He knew that if he let, for an instant, to secure a better mouthful, his enemy would escape; so he just worried and chewed at the joint, satisfied with the punishment he was inflicting.

Meanwhile, the woodsman, his attention drawn by that one sudden yelp of the falcon and by the prolonged and violent buffeting of wings, had turned back to see what was going on. Pausing at the foot of Mustela's tree, he peered upwards with narrowed eyes. A slow smile wrinkled his weather-beaten face. He did not like hawks. For a moment or two he stood wondering what it was in the hole that could hold so powerful a bird. Whatever it was, he stood for it.

Being a dead shot with the revolver, he seldom troubled to carry a rifle in his 'cruisings'. Drawing his long-barrelled 'Smith and Wesson' from his belt, he took careful aim and fired. At the sound of the shot, the thing in the hole was startled and let go; and the great bird, turning once over slowly in the air, dropped to his feet with a feathery thud, its talons still contracting shudderingly. The woodsman glanced lip, and there, framed in the dark of the hole, was the little yellow face of Mustela, insatiably curious, snarling down upon him viciously.

'Gee,' muttered the woodsman, 'I might hev' knowed it was one o' them pesky martens! Nobody else o' *that* size 'd hev' the gall to tackle a duck-hawk!'

Now, the fur of Mustela, the pine-marten or American sable, is a fur of price; but the woodsman—subject, like most of his kind, to unexpected attacks of sentiment and imagination—felt that to shoot the defiant little fighter would be like an act of treachery to an ally.

'Ye're a pretty fighter, sonny,' said he, with a whimsical grin, 'an' ye may keep that yaller pelt o' yourn, for all o' me!' Then he picked up the dead falcon, tied its claws together, slung it upon his axe, and strode off through the trees. He wanted to keep those splendid wings as a present for his girl in at the settlements.

Highly satisfied with his victory over the mighty falcon—for which he took the full credit to himself—Mustela now retired to the bottom of his comfortable, moss-lined nest and curled himself up to sleep away the heat of the day. As the heat grew sultrier and drowsier through the still hours of early afternoon, there fell upon the forest a heavy silence, deepened rather than broken by the faint hum of the heat-loving flies. And the spicy scents of pine and spruce and tamarack steamed forth richly upon the moveless air.

When the shadows of the trunks began to lengthen, Mustela woke up, and he woke up hungry. Slipping out of his hole, he ran a little way down the trunk and then leapt, lightly and nimbly as a squirrel, into the branches of a big hemlock which grew close to his own tree. Here, in a crotch from which he commanded a good view beneath the foliage, he halted and stood motionless, peering about him for some sign of a likely quarry.

Poised thus, tense, erect and vigilant, Mustela was a picture of beauty, swift and fierce. In colour he was of a rich golden-brown, with a patch of brilliant yellow covering throat and chest. His tail was long and bushy, to serve him as a balance in his long, squirrel-like leaps from tree to tree. His pointed ears were large and alert, to catch all the faint, elusive forest sounds. In length, being a specially fine specimen of his kind, he was perhaps a couple of inches over two feet. His body had all the lithe grace of a weasel, with something of the strength of his great-cousin and most dreaded foe, the fisher.

For a time nothing stirred. Then from a distance came, faint but shrill, the chirr-r-r-r of a red squirrel. Mustela's discriminating ear located the sound at once. All energy on the instant, he darted towards it, springing from branch to branch with amazing speed and noiselessness.

The squirrel, noisy and imprudent after the manner of his tribe, was chattering fussily and bouncing about on his branch, excited over something best known to himself, when a darting, gold-brown shape of doom landed upon the other end of the branch, not half a dozen feet from him. With a screech of warning and terror, he bounded into the air, alighted on the trunk and raced up it, with Mustela close upon his heels. Swift as he was—and everyone who has seen a red squirrel in a hurry knows how he can move—Mustela was swifter, and in about five seconds the little chatterer's fate would have been sealed. But he knew what he was about. This was his own tree. Had it been otherwise, he would have sprung into another, and directed his desperate flight over the slenderest branches, where his enemy's greater weight would be a hindrance. As it was, he managed to gain his hole—just in time—and all that Mustela got was a little mouthful of fur from the tip of that vanishing red tail. Very angry and disappointed, and hissing like a cat, Mustela jammed his savage face into the hole. He could see the squirrel crouched, with pounding heart and panic-stricken eyes, a few inches below him, just out of his reach. The hole was too small to admit his head. In a rage he tore at the edges with his powerful claws, but the wood was too hard for him to make any impression on it, and after half a minute of futile scratching, he gave up in disgust and raced off down the tree. A moment later the squirrel poked his head out and shrieked an effectual warning to every creature within earshot.

With that loud alarm shrilling in his ears, Mustela knew there would be no successful hunting for him till he could put himself beyond the range of it. He raced on, therefore, abashed by his failure, till the taunting sound faded in the distance. Then his bushy brown brush went up in the air again, and his wonted look of insolent self-confidence returned. As it did not seem to be his lucky day for squirrels, he descended to earth and began quartering the ground for the fresh trail of a rabbit.

In that section of the forest where Mustela now found himself, the dark and scented tangle of spruce and balsam-fir was broken by thickets of stony barren, clothed unevenly by thickets of stunted white birch, and silver-leaved quaking aspen, and wild sumach with its massive tufts of acrid, dark-crimson bloom. Here the rabbit trails were abundant, and Mustela was not long in finding one fresh enough to offer him the prospect of a speedy kill. Swiftly and silently, nose to earth, he set himself to follow its intricate and apparently aimless windings, sure that he would come upon a rabbit at the end of it.

As it chanced, however, he never came to the end of that particular trail or set his teeth in the throat of that particular rabbit. In gliding past a bushy young fir-tree, he happened to glance be path it, and marked another of his tribe tearing the feathers from a new-slain grouse. The stranger was smaller and slighter than himself—a young female—quite possibly, indeed, his mate of a few months earlier in the season. Such considerations were less than nothing to Mustela, whose ferocious spirit knew neither gallantry, chivalry, nor mercy. With what seemed a single flashing leap, he was upon her—or almost, for the slim female was no longer there. She had bounded away as lightly and instantaneously as if blown by the wind of his coming. She knew Mustela, and she knew it would be death to stay and do battle for her kill. Spitting with rage and fear, she fled from the spot, terrified lest he should pursue her and find the nest where her six precious kittens were concealed.

But Mustela was too hungry to be interested just then in mere slaughter for its own sake. He was feeling serious and practical. The grouse was a full-grown cock, plump and juicy, and when Mustela had devoured it, his appetite was sated. But not so his blood-lust. After a hasty toilet he set out again, looking for something to kill.

Crossing the belt of rocky ground, he emerged upon a flat tract of treeless barren covered with a dense growth of blueberry bushes about a foot in height. The bushes at this season were loaded with ripe fruit of a bright blue colour, and squatting among them was a big black bear, enjoying the banquet at his ease. Gathering the berries together, wholesale with his great furry paws, he was cramming them into his mouth greedily, with little grunts and gurgles of delight, and the juicy fragments with which his snout and jaws were smeared, gave his formidable face an absurdly childish look. To Mustela—when that insolent little animal flashed before him—he vouchsafed no more than a glance of good-natured contempt. For the rank and stringy flesh of a pine-marten he had no use at any time of the year, least of all in the season when the blueberries were ripe.

Mustela, however, was too discreet to pass within reach of one of those huge but nimble paws, lest the happy bear should grow playful under the stimulus of the blueberry juice. He turned aside to a judicious distance, and there, sitting up on his hindquarters like a rabbit, he proceeded to nibble, rather superciliously, a few of the choicest berries. He was not enthusiastic over vegetable food, but, just as a cat will now and then eat grass, he liked at times a little corrective to his unvarying diet of flesh.

Having soon had enough of the blueberry patch, Mustela left it to the bear and turned back toward the deep of the forest, where he felt most at home. He went stealthily, following up the wind in order that his scent might not give warning of his approach. It was getting near sunset by this time, and floods of pinky gold, washing across the open barrens, poured in along the ancient corridors of the forest, touching the sombre trunks with stains of tenderest rose. In this glowing colour Mustela, with his ruddy fur, moved almost invisible.

And, so moving, he came plump upon a big buck-rabbit squatting half-asleep in the centre of a clump of pale green fern.

The rabbit hounded straight into the air, his big, childish eyes popping from his head with horror. Mustela's leap was equally instantaneous, and it was unerring. He struck his victim in mid-air, and his fangs met deep in the rabbit's throat. With a scream the rabbit fell backwards and came down with a muffled thump upon the ferns, with Mustela on top of him. There was a brief, thrashing struggle, and then Mustela, his forepaws upon the breast of his still quivering prey—several times larger and heavier than himself—lifted his blood-stained face and stared about him savagely, as if defying all the other prowlers of the forest to come and try to rob him of his prize.

Having eaten his fill, Mustela dragged the remnants of the carcass under a thick bush, defiled it so as to make it distasteful to other eaters of flesh, and scratched a lot of dead leaves and twigs over it till it was effectually hidden. As game was abundant at this season, and as he always preferred a fresh kill, he was not likely to want any more of that victim, but he hated the thought of any rival getting a profit from his prowess.

Mustela now turned his steps homeward, travelling more lazily, but with eyes, nose and ears ever on the alert for fresh quarry. Though his appetite was sated for some hours, he was as eager as ever for the hunt, for the fierce joy of the killing and the taste of the hot blood. But the unseen powers of the wilderness, ironic and impartial, decided just then that it was time for Mustela to be hunted in his turn.

If there was one creature above all others who could strike the fear of death into Mustela's merciless soul, it was his great-cousin, the ferocious and implacable fisher. Of twice his weight and thrice his strength, and his full peer in swiftness and cunning, the fisher was Mustela's nightmare, from whom there was no escape unless in the depths of some hole too narrow for the fisher's powerful shoulders to get into. And at this moment there was the fisher's grinning, black-muzzled mask crouched in the path before him, eyeing him with the sneer of certain triumph.

Mustela's heart jumped into his throat as he flashed about and fled for his life—straight away, alas, from his safe hole in the tree-top—and with the lightning dart of a striking rattler the fisher was after him.

Mustela had a start of perhaps twenty paces, and for a time he held his own. He dared no tricks, lest he should lose ground, for he knew his foe was as swift and as cunning as himself. But he knew himself stronger and more enduring than most of his tribe, and therefore he put his hope, for the most part, in his endurance. Moreover, there was always a chance that he might come upon some hole or crevice too narrow for his pursuer. Indeed, to a tough and indomitable spirit like Mustela's, until his enemy's fangs should finally lock themselves in his throat, there would always seem to be a chance. One could never know which way the freakish Fates of the wilderness would cast their favour. On and on he raced, therefore, tearing up or down the long, sloping trunks of ancient windfalls, twisting like a golden snake through tangled thickets, springing in great airy leaps from trunk to rock, from rock to overhanging branch, in silence; and ever at his heels followed the relentless, grinning shape of his pursuer, gaining a little in the long leaps, but losing a little in the denser thickets, and so just about keeping his distance.

For all Mustela's endurance, the end of that race, in all

probability, would have been for him but one swift, screeching fight, and then the dark. But at this juncture the Fates woke up, peered ironically through the grey and ancient mosses of their hair, and remembered some grudge against the fisher.

A moment later, Mustela, just launching himself on a desperate leap, beheld in his path a huge hornets nest suspended from a branch near the ground. Well he knew, and respected, that terrible insect, the great black hornet with the cream-white stripes about his body. But it was too late to turn aside. He crashed against the grey, papery sphere, tearing it from its cables, and flashed on, with half a dozen white-hot stings in his hindquarters prodding him to a fresh burst of speed. Swerving slightly, he dashed through a dense thicket of juniper scrub, hoping not only to scrape his fiery tormentors off, but at the same time to gain a little on his big pursuer.

The fisher was at this stage not more than a dozen paces in the rear. He arrived, to his undoing, just as the outraged hornets poured out in a furiously humming swarm from their overturned nest. It was clear enough to them that the fisher was their assailant. With deadly unanimity they pouched upon him.

With a startled screech the fisher bounced aside and plunged for shelter. But he was too late. The great hornets were all over him. His ears and nostrils were black with them, his long fur was full of them, and his eyes, shut tight, were already a flaming anguish with the corroding poison of their stings. Frantically he burrowed his face down into the moss and through into the moist earth, and madly he clawed at his ears, crushing scores of his tormentors. But he could not crush out the venom which their long stings had injected. Finding it hopeless to free himself from their swarms, he tore madly through the underbrush, but blindly, crashing into trunks and rocks, heedless of everything but the fiery torture which enveloped him. Gradually the hornets fell away from him as he went, knowing that their vengeance was accomplished. At last, groping his way blindly into a crevice between two rocks, he thrust his head down into the moss, and there, a few days later, his swollen body was found by a foraging lynx. The lynx was hungry, but she only sniffed at the carcass and turned away with a growl of disappointment and suspicion. The carcass was too full of poison even for her not-too-discriminating palate.

Mustela, meanwhile, having the best and sharpest of reasons for not delaying in his flight, knew nothing of the fate of his pursuer. He only became aware, after some minutes, that he was no longer pursued. Incredulous at first, he at length came to the conclusion that the fisher had been discouraged by his superior speed and endurance. His heart, though still pounding unduly, swelled with triumph. By way of precaution he made a long detour to come back to his nest, pounced upon and devoured a couple of plump deer mice on the way, ran up his tree and slipped comfortably into his hole, and curled up to sleep with the feeling of a day well spent. He had fed full, he had robbed his fellows successfully, he had drunk the blood of his victims, he had outwitted or eluded his enemies. As for his friends, he had none—a fact which to Mustela of the Lone Hand was of no concern whatever.

Now, as the summer waned, and the first keen touch of autumn set the wilderness aflame with the scarlet of maple and sumach, the pale gold of poplar and birch, Mustela, for all his abounding health and prosperous hunting, grew restless with a discontent which he could not understand. Of the coming winter he had no dread. He had passed through several winters, faring well when other prowlers less daring and expert had starved, and finding that deep nest of his in the old tree a snug refuge from the fiercest storms. But now—he knew not why—the nest grew irksome to him, and his familiar hunting-grounds distasteful. Even the eager hunt, the triumphant kill itself, had lost their zest. He forgot to kill except when he was hungry. A strange fever was in his blood, a lust for wandering. And so, one wistful, softly-glowing day of Indian summer, when the violet light that bathed the forest was full of mystery and allurement, he set off on a journey. He had no thought of why he was going, or whither. Nor was he conscious of any haste. When hungry, he stopped to hunt and kill and feed. But he no longer cared to conceal the remnants of his kills, for he dimly realized that he would not be returning. If running waters crossed his path, he swam them. If broad lakes intervened, he skirted them. From time to time he became aware that others of his kind were moving with him, but each one furtive, silent, solitary, self-sufficing, like himself. He heeded them not, nor they him; but all, impelled by one urge which could but be blindly obeyed, kept drifting onward toward the west and north. At length, when the first snows began, Mustela stopped, in a forest not greatly different from that which he had left, but ever wilder, denser, more unvisited by the foot of man. And here, the wanderlust having suddenly left his blood, he found himself a new hole, lined it warm with moss and dry grasses, and resumed his hunting with all the ancient zest. Back in Mustela's old hunting-grounds a lonely trapper, finding no more golden sable in his snares, but only mink and lynx and fox, grumbled regretfully:

'The marten hev quit. We'll see no more of 'em round these parts for another ten year.'

But he had no notion why they had quit, nor had anyone else—not even Mustela himself.

BECKWITH'S CASE

Maurice Hewlett

The facts were as follows. Mr Stephen Mortimer Beckwith was a young man living at Wilsford in the Amesbury district of Wiltshire. He was a clerk in the Wilts and Dorset Bank at Salisbury, was married and had one child. His age at the time of the experience here related was twenty-eight. His health was excellent.

On 30 November 1887, at about ten o'clock at night, he was returning home from Amesbury, where he had been spending the evening at a friend's house. The weather was mild, with a rain-bearing wind blowing in squalls from the south-west. It was three-quarter moon that night, and although the sky was frequently overcast, it was at no time dark. Mr Beckwith, who was riding a bicycle and accompanied by his Fox-terrier, Strap, states that he had no difficulty in seeing and avoiding the stones cast down at intervals by the road-menders; that flocks of sheep in the hollows were very visible, and that passing Wilsford House he saw a barn owl quite plainly and remarked its heavy, uneven flight.

A mile beyond Wilsford House, Strap, the dog, broke through the quickset hedge upon his right-hand side and ran yelping up the down, which rises sharply just there. Mr

Beckwith, who imagined that he was after a hare, whistled him in, presently calling him sharply, 'Strap, Strap, come out of it.' The dog took no notice, but ran directly to a clump of gorse and bramble halfway up the down, and stood there in the attitude of a pointer, with uplifted paw, watching the gorse intently, and whining. Mr Beckwith was by this time dismounted, observing the dog. He watched him for some minutes from the road. The moon was bright, the sky at the moment free from cloud.

He himself could see nothing in the gorse, though the dog was undoubtedly in a high state of excitement. It made frequent rushes forward, but stopped short of the object that it saw and trembled. It did not bark outright, but rather whimpered—'a curious, shuddering crying noise', says Mr Beckwith. Interested by the animal's persistent and singular behaviour, he now sought a gap in the hedge, went through on to the down and approached the clumped bushes. Strap was so much occupied that he barely noticed his master's coming; it seemed as if he dared not take his eyes off for one second from what he saw in there.

Beckwith, standing behind the dog, looked into the gorse. From the distance at which he stood, still he could see nothing at all. His belief then was that there was either a tramp in a drunken sleep, possibly two tramps, or a hare caught in a wire, or possibly even a fox. Having no stick with him, he did not care, at first, to go any nearer, and contented himself with urging on the Terrier. This was not very courageous of him, as he admits, and was quite unsuccessful. No verbal excitations could draw Strap nearer to the furze-bush. Finally the dog threw up his head, showed his master the white arcs of his eyes and fairly howled at the moon. At this dismal sound Mr Beckwith was himself alarmed. It was, as he describes it—though he is an Englishman—'uncanny'. The time, he owns, the aspect of the night, loneliness of the spot (midway up the steep slope of a chalk down), the mysterious shroud of darkness upon shadowed and distant objects, and flood of white light upon the foreground—all these circumstances worked upon his imagination.

He was indeed for retreat; but here Strap was of a different mind. Nothing would excite him to advance, but nothing, either, could induce him to retire. Whatever he saw in the furze-bush Strap must continue to observe. In the face of this, Beckwith summoned up his courage, took it in both hands and went much nearer to the furze-bushes, much nearer, that is, than Strap the Terrier could bring himself to go. Then, he tells us, he did see a pair of bright eyes far in the thicket, which seemed to be fixed upon his, and by degrees also a pale and troubled face. Here, then, was neither fox nor drunken tramp, but some human creature, man, woman, or child, fully aware of him and of the dog.

Beckwith, who now had surer command of his feelings, spoke aloud, asking, 'What are you doing there? What's the matter?' He had no reply. He went one pace nearer, being still on his guard, and spoke again. 'I won't hurt you,' he said. 'Tell me what the matter is.' The eyes remained unwinkingly fixed upon his own. No movement of the features could be discerned. The face, as he could now make it out, was very small—'about as big as a big wax dolls,' he says, 'of a longish oval, very pale.' He adds, 'I could see its neck now, no thicker than my wrist; and where its clothes began, I couldn't see any arms, for a good reason. I found out afterwards that they had been bound behind its back. I should have said immediately, "That's a girl in there", if it had not been for one or two plain considerations. It had not the size of what we call a girl, nor the face of what we mean by a child. It was, in fact, neither fish, flesh, nor fowl. Strap had known that from the beginning, and now I was of Strap's opinion myself.'

Advancing with care, a step at a time, Beckwith presently found himself within touching distance of the creature. He was now standing with furze halfway up his calves, right above it, stooping to look closely at it; and as he stooped and moved now this way, now that, to get a clearer view, so the crouching thing's eyes gazed up to meet his, and followed them about, as if safety lay only in that never-shifting, fixed regard. He had noticed, and states in his narrative, that Strap had seemed quite unable, in the same way, to take his eyes off the creature for a single second.

He could now see that, of whatever nature it might be, it was in form and features, most exactly a young woman. The features, for instance, were regular and fine. He remarks in particular upon the chin. All about its face, narrowing the oval of it, fell dark, glossy curtains of hair, very straight and glistening with wet. Its garment was cut in a plain circle round the neck and shorn off at the shoulders, leaving the arms entirely bare. This garment, shift, smock or gown, as he indifferently calls it, appeared thin, and was found afterwards to be of a grey colour, soft and clinging to the shape. It was made loose, however, and gathered in at the waist. He could not see the creature's legs as they were tucked under her. Her arms, it has been related, were behind her back. The only other things to be remarked upon were the strange stillness of one who was plainly suffering, and might well be alarmed, an appearance of expectancy, a dumb appeal; what he himself calls rather well 'an ignorant sort of impatience, like that of a sick animal'.

'Come,' Beckwith now said, 'let me help you up. You will

get cold if you sit here. Give me your hand, will you?' She neither spoke nor moved; simply continued to search his eyes. Strap, meantime, was still trembling and whining. But now, when he stooped yet lower to take her forcibly by the arms, she shrank back a little way and turned her head, and he saw to his horror that she had a great open wound in the side of her neck—from which, however, no blood was issuing. Yet it was clearly a fresh wound, recently made.

He was greatly shocked. 'Good God,' he said, 'there's been foul play here,' and whipped out his handkerchief. Kneeling, he wound it several times round her slender throat and knotted it as tightly as he could; then, without more ado, he took her up in his arms, under the knees and round the middle, and carried her down the slope to the road. He describes her as of no weight at all. He says it was 'exactly like carrying an armful of feathers about'. 'I took her down the hill and through the hedge at the bottom as if she had been a pillow.'

Here it was that he discovered that her wrists were bound together behind her back with a kind of plait of things so intricate that he was quite unable to release them. He felt his pockets for his knife, but could not find it, and then recollected suddenly that he should have a new one with him, the third prize in a whist tournament in which he had taken part that evening. He found it wrapped in paper in his overcoat pocket, with it cut the thongs and set the little creature free. She immediately responded—the first sign of animation which she had displayed by throwing both her arms about his body and clinging to him in an ecstasy. Holding him so that, as he says, he felt the shuddering go all through her, she suddenly lowered her head and touched his wrist with her cheek. He says that instead of being cold to the touch, 'like a fish', as she had seemed to be when he first took her out of the gorse, she was now 'as warm as toast, like a child.'

So far he had put her down for 'a foreigner', convenient term for defining something which one does not quite understand. She had none of his language, evidently; she was undersized, some, three feet six inches, by the look of her, and yet perfectly proportioned. She was most curiously dressed in a frock cut to the knee, and actually in nothing else at all. It left her barelegged and bare-armed, and was made, as he puts it himself, of stuff like cobweb, 'those dusty, drooping kind which you put on your finger to stop bleeding'. He could not recognize the web, but was sure that it was neither linen nor cotton. It seemed to stick to her body wherever it touched a prominent part. 'You could see very well, to say nothing of feeling, that she was well-made and well-nourished.' She ought, as he judged, to be a child of five years old, 'and a feather-weight at that'; but he felt certain that she must be 'much more like sixteen'. It was that, I gather, which made him suspect her of being something outside experience. So far, then, it was safe to call her a foreigner: but he was not yet at the end of his discoveries.

Heavy footsteps, coming from the direction of Wilsford, in due time proved to be of Police Constable Gulliver, a neighbour of Beckwith's and guardian of the peace in his own village. He lifted his lantern to flash it into the traveller's eyes, and dropped it again with a pleasant 'good evening'. He added that it was inclined to be showery, which was more than true, as it was, at the moment, raining hard. With that, it seems, he would have passed on.

But Beckwith, whether smitten by self-consciousness of having been seen with a young woman in his arms at a suspicious hour of the night by the village policeman, or bursting perhaps with the importance of his affair, detained Gulliver. 'Just look at this,' he said boldly. 'Here's a pretty thing to have found on a lonely road. Foul play somewhere, I'm afraid;' he then exhibited his burden to the lantern light.

To his extreme surprise, however, the constable, after exploring the beam of light and all that it contained for some time in silence, reached out his hand for the knife which Beckwith still held open. He looked at it on both sides, examined the handle and gave it back. 'Foul play, Mr Beckwith?' he said, laughing. 'Bless you, they use bigger tools than that. That's just a toy, the like of that. Cut your hand with it, though, already, I see.' He must have noticed the handkerchief, for as he spoke the light from his lantern shone full upon the face and neck of the child, or creature, in the young man's arms, so clearly that, looking down at it, Beckwith himself could see the clear grey of its intensely watchful eyes, and the very pupils of them, diminished to specks of black. It was now, therefore, plain to him that what he held was a foreigner indeed, since the parish constable was unable to see it. Strap had smelt it, then seen it, and he, Beckwith, had seen it; but it was invisible to Gulliver. 'I felt now,' he says in his narrative, 'that something was wrong. I did not like the idea of taking it into the house; but I intended to make one more trial before I made up my mind about that. I said good night to Gulliver, put her on my bicycle and pushed her home. But first of all I took the handkerchief from her neck and put it in my pocket. There was no blood upon it, that I could see.'

His wife, as he had expected, was waiting at the gate for him. She exclaimed, as he had expected, upon the lateness of the hour. Beckwith stood for a little in the roadway before the house, explaining that Strap had bolted up the hill and had to be looked for and fetched back. While speaking he noticed that Mrs Beckwith was as insensible to the creature on the bicycle as Gulliver the constable had been. Indeed, she went much farther to prove herself so than he, for she actually put her hand upon the handle-bar of the machine, and in order to that drove it right through the centre of the girl crouching there. Beckwith saw that done. 'I declare solemnly upon my honour,' he writes, 'that it was as if Mary had drilled a hole clean through the middle of her back. Through gown and skin and bone and all her arm went; and how it went in I don't know. To me it seemed that her hand was on the handle-bar, while her upper arm, to the elbow, was in between the girl's shoulders. There was a gap from the elbow downwards where Mary's arm was inside the body; then from the creature's diaphragm her lower arm, wrist and hand came out. And all the time we were speaking the girl's eyes were on my face. I was now quite determined that I wouldn't have her in the house for a mint of money.'

He put her, finally, in the dog-kennel. Strap, as a favourite, lived in the house; but he kept a Greyhound in the garden, in a kennel surrounded by a sort of run made of iron poles and galvanized wire. It was roofed in with wire also, for the convenience of stretching a tarpaulin in wet weather. Here it was that he bestowed the strange being rescued from the down. It was clever, I think, of Beckwith to infer that what Strap had shown respect for would be respected by the Greyhound, and certainly bold of him to act upon his inference. However, events proved that he had been perfectly right. Bran, the Greyhound, was interested, highly interested, in his guest. The moment he saw his master, he saw what he was carrying. 'Quiet, Bran, quiet there,' was a very unnecessary adjuration. Bran stretched up his head and sniffed, but went no farther; and when Beckwith had placed his burden on the straw inside the kennel, Bran lay down, as if on guard, outside the opening and put his muzzle on his forepaws. Again Beckwith noticed that curious appearance of the eyes which the Fox-terrier's had made already. Bran's eyes were turned upwards to show the narrow arcs of white.

Before he went to bed, he tells us, but not before Mrs Beckwith had gone there, he took out a bowl of bread and milk to his patient. Bran, he found to be still stretched out before the entry; the girl was nestled down in the straw, as if asleep or prepared to be so, with her face upon her hand. Upon an afterthought he went back for a clean pocket handkerchief, warm water and a sponge. With these, by the light of a candle, he washed the wound, dipped the rag in hazeline and applied it. This done, he touched the creature's head, nodded a good night and retired. 'She smiled at me very prettily,' he says. 'That was the first time she did it.'

There was no blood on the handkerchief which he had removed.

Early in the morning, following upon the adventure, Beckwith was out and about. He wished to verify the overnight experiences in the light of refreshed intelligence. On approaching the kennel he saw at once that it had been no dream. There, in fact, was the creature of his discovery playing with Bran the Greyhound, circling sedately about him, weaving her arms, pointing her toes, arching her graceful neck, stooping to him, as if inviting him to sport, darting away—'like a fairy,' says Beckwith, 'at her magic, dancing in a ring.' Bran, he observed, made no effort to catch her, but crouched rather than sat, as if ready to spring. He followed her about with his eyes as far as he could; but when the course of her dance took her immediately behind him, he did not turn his head, but kept his eye fixed as far backward as he could, against the moment when she should come again into the scope of his vision. 'It seemed as important to him, as it had the day before to Strap, to keep her always in his eye. It seemed—and always seemed so long as I could study them together—intensely important.' Bran's mouth was stretched to 'a sort of grin'; occasionally he panted. When Beckwith entered the kennel and touched the dog (which took little notice of him), he found him trembling with excitement. His heart was heating at a great rate. He also drank quantities of water.

Beckwith, whose narrative, hitherto summarized, I may now quote, tells us that 'the creature was indescribably graceful and lightfooted. You couldn't hear the fall of her foot: you never could. Her dancing and circling about the cage seemed to be the most important business of her life; she was always at it, especially in bright weather. I shouldn't have called it restlessness so much as busyness. It really seemed to mean more to her than exercise or irritation at confinement. It was evident also that she was happy when so engaged. She used to sing. She sang also when she was sitting still with Bran; but not with such exhilaration.

'Her eyes were bright—when she was dancing about—with mischief and devilry. I cannot avoid that word, thought it does not describe what I really mean. She looked wild and outlandish and full of fun, as if she knew that she was teasing the dog, and yet couldn't help herself. When you say of a child that he looks wicked, you don't mean it literally; it is rather a compliment than not. So it was with her and her wickedness. She did look wicked, there's no mistake—able and willing to do wickedness; but I am sure she never meant to hurt Bran. They were always firm friends, though the dog knew very well who was the master.

'When you looked at her you did not think of her height. She was so complete; as well-made as a statuette. I could have spanned her waist with my two thumbs and middle fingers, and her neck (very nearly) with one hand. She was pale and inclined to be dusky in complexion, but not so dark as a gypsy; she had grey eyes, and dark brown hair, which she could sit upon if she chose. Her gown you could have sworn was made of cobweb; I don't know how else to describe it. As I had suspected, she wore nothing else, for while I was there that first morning, so soon as the sun came up over the hill she slipped it off her and stood dressed in nothing at all. She was a regular little Venus, that's all I can say. I never could get accustomed to that weakness of hers for slipping off her frock, though no doubt it was very absurd. She had no sort of shame in it, so why on earth should I?

'The food, I ought to mention, had disappeared: the bowl was empty. But I know now that Bran must have had it. So long as she remained in the kennel or about my place she never ate anything, nor drank either. If she had I must have known it, as I used to clean the run out every morning. I was always particular about that. I used to say that you couldn't keep dogs too clean. But I tried her unsuccessfully, with all sorts of things: flowers, honey, dew—for I had read somewhere that fairies drink dew and suck honey out of flowers. She used to look at the little messes I made for her, and when she knew me better, would grimace at them, and look up in my face and laugh at me.

'I have said that she used to sing sometimes. It was like nothing that I can describe. Perhaps the wind in the telegraph wires comes nearest to it, and yet that is an absurd comparison. I could never catch any words; indeed I did not succeed in learning a single word of her language. I doubt very much whether they have what we call a language—I mean, the people who are like her, her own people. They communicate with each other, I fancy, as she did with my dogs, inarticulately, but with perfect communication and understanding on either side. When I began to teach her English, I noticed that she had a kind of pity for me, a kind of contempt perhaps is nearer the mark, that I should be compelled to express myself in so clumsy a way. I am no philosopher, but I imagine that our need of putting one word after another may be due to our habit of thinking in sequence. If there is no such thing as time in the other world, it should not be necessary there to frame speech in sentences at all. I am sure that Thumbeline (which was my name for her; I never learned her real name) spoke with Bran and Strap in flashes, which revealed her whole thought at once. So also they answered her, there's no doubt. So also she contrived to talk with my little girl, who, although she was four years old and a great chatterbox, never attempted to say a single word of her own language to Thumbeline, yet communicated with her by the hour together. But I did not know anything of this for a month or more, though it must have begun almost at once.

'I blame myself for it, myself only. I ought, of course, to have remembered that children are more likely to see fairies than grownups; but then—why did Florrie keep it all a secret? Why did she not tell her mother, or me, that she had seen a fairy in Bran's kennel? The child was as open as the day, yet she concealed her knowledge from both of us without the least difficulty. She seemed the same careless, laughing child she had always been; one could not have supposed her to have a care in the world; and yet for nearly six months she must have been full of care, having daily secret intercourse with Thumbeline and keeping her eyes open all the time lest her mother or I should find her out. Certainly she could have taught me something in the way of keeping secrets. I know that I kept mine very badly, and blame myself more than enough for keeping it at all. God knows what we might have been spared, if, on the night I brought her home, I had told Mary the whole truth! And yet how could I have convinced her that she was impaling someone with her arm while her hand rested on the bar of the bicycle? Is not that an absurdity on the face of it? Yes, indeed; but the sequel is no absurdity. That's the terrible fact.

'I kept Thumbeline in the kennel for the whole winter. She seemed happy enough there with the dogs, and, of course, she had had Florrie, too, though I did not find that out until the spring. I don't doubt, now, that if I had kept her in there altogether, she would have been perfectly contented.

'The first time I saw Florrie with her, I was amazed. It was a Sunday morning. There was our four-year-old child standing at the wire, pressing herself against it, and Thumbeline close to her. Their faces almost touched; their fingers were interlaced; I am certain that they were speaking to each other in their own fashion, by flashes, without words. I watched them for a bit; I saw Bran come and sit up on his haunches and join them. He looked from one to another, and all about; and then he saw me.

'Now that is how I know that they were all three in communication, because, the very next moment, Florrie turned round and ran to me, and said in her pretty baby-talk, "Talking to Bran. Florrie talking to Bran." If this was willful deceit, it was most accomplished. It could not have been better done. "And who else were you talking to, Florrie?" I said. She fixed her round blue eyes upon me, and said shortly, "No one else." And I could not get her to confess or admit, then or at any time afterwards, that she had any cognizance at all of the fairy in Bran's kennel, although their communications were daily, and often lasted for hours at a time. I don't know that it makes things any better, but I have thought sometimes that the child believed me to be as insensible to Thumbeline as her mother was. She can only have believed it at first, of course, but that may have prompted her to a concealment which she did not afterwards care to confess to.

'Be this as it may, Florrie, in fact, behaved with Thumbeline exactly as the two dogs did. She made no attempt to catch her at her circlings and wheelings about the kennel, nor to follow her wonderful dances, nor (in her presence) to imitate them. But she was (like the dogs) aware of nobody else when under the spell of Thumbeline's personality; and when she had got to know her, she seemed to care for nobody else at all. I ought, no doubt, to have foreseen that and guarded against it.

'Thumbeline was extremely attractive. I never saw such eyes as hers, such mysterious fascination. She was nearly always good-tempered, nearly always happy; but sometimes she had fits of temper and kept herself to herself. Nothing then would get her out of the kennel, where she would lie curled up like an animal with her knees to her chin and one arm thrown over her face. Bran was always wretched at these times, and did all he knew to coax her out. He ceased to care for me or my wife after she came to us, and instead of being wild at the prospect of his Saturday and Sunday runs, it was hard to get him along. I had to take him on a leash until we had turned to go home; then he would set off by himself, in spite of hallooing and scolding, at a long steady gallop, and one would find him waiting crouched at the gate of his run, and Thumbeline on the ground inside it, with her legs crossed like tailor, mocking and teasing him with her wonderful shining eyes. Only once or twice did I see her worse than sick or sorry; then she was transported with rage and another person altogether. She never touched me—and why or how I had offended her I have no notion—but she buzzed and hovered about me like an angry bee. She appeared to have wings, which hummed in their furious movement; she was red in the face; her eyes burned; she grinned at me and ground her little teeth together. A curious shrill noise came from her, like the screaming of a gnat or hover-fly; but no words, never any words. Bran showed me his teeth too, and would not look at me. It was very odd.

'When I looked in, on my return home, she was as merry as usual, and as affectionate. I think she had no memory.

'I am trying to give all the particulars I was able to gather from my observation. In some things she was difficult, in others very easy to teach. For instance, I got her to learn in no time that she ought to wear her clothes, such as they were, when I was with her. She certainly preferred to go without them, especially in the sunshine; but by leaving her, the moment she slipped her frock off, I soon made her understand that if she wanted me she must behave herself according to my notions of behaviour. She got that fixed in her little head, but even so she used to do her best to hoodwink me. She would slip out one shoulder when she thought I wasn't looking, and before I knew where I was, half of her would be gleaming in the sun like satin. Directly I noticed it I used to frown, and then she would pretend to be ashamed of herself, hang her head and wriggle her frock up to its place again. However, I could never teach her to keep her skirts about her knees. She was as innocent as a baby about that sort of thing.

'I taught her some English words, and a sentence or two. That was towards the end of her confinement to the kennel, about March. I used to touch parts of her, or of myself, or Bran, and peg away at the names of them. Mouth, eyes, ears, hands, chest, tail, back, front: she learned all those and more. Eat, drink, laugh, cry, love, kiss, those also. As for kissing (apart from the word) she proved herself to be an expert. She kissed me, Florrie, Bran, Strap, indifferently, one as soon as another, and any rather than none, and all four for choice.

'I learned some things myself, more than a thing or two. I don't mind owning that one thing was to value my wife's steady and tried affection far above the wild love of this unbalanced, unearthly little creature, who seemed to be like nothing so much as a woman with the conscience left out. The conscience, we believe, is the still small voice of the Deity crying to us in the dark recesses of the body; pointing out the path of duty; teaching respect for the opinion of the world, for tradition, decency and order. It is thanks to conscience that a man is true and a woman modest. Not that Thumbeline could be called immodest, unless a baby can be so described or an animal. But could I be called true? I greatly fear that I could not—in fact, I know it too well. I meant no harm; I was greatly interested; and there was always before me the real difficulty of making Mary understand that something was in the kennel which she couldn't see. It would have led to great complications, even if I had persuaded her of the fact. No doubt she would have insisted on my getting rid of Thumbeline—but how on earth could I have done that if Thumbeline had not chosen to go? But, for all that, I know very well that I ought to have told her, cost what it might. If I had done it I should have spared myself lifelong regret, and should only have gone without a few weeks of extraordinary interest, which I now see clearly could not have been good for me, as not being founded upon any revealed Christian principle, and most certainly were not worth the price I had to pay for them.

'I learned one more curious fact which I must not forget. Nothing would induce Thumbeline to touch or pass over anything made of zinc. I don't know the reason for it; but gardeners will tell you that the way to keep a plant from slugs is to put a zinc collar round it. It is due to that I was able to keep her in Bran's run without difficulty. To have got out she would have had to pass zinc. The wire was all galvanized.

'She showed her dislike of it in numerous ways: one was her care to avoid touching the sides or tops of the enclosure when she was at her gambols. At such times, when she was at her wildest, she was all over the place, skipping high like a lamb, twisting like a leveret, wheeling round and round in circles like a young dog, or skimming, like a swallow on the wing, above ground. But she never made a mistake; she turned in a moment or flung herself backward if there was the least risk of contact. When Florrie used to converse with her from outside, in that curious silent way the two had, it would always be the child that put its hands through the wire, never Thumbeline. I once tried to put her against the roof when I was playing with her. She screamed like a shot hare and would not come out of the kennel all day. There was no doubt at all about her feelings for zinc. All other metals seemed indifferent to her.

'With the advent of spring weather, Thumbeline became not only more beautiful, but wilder, and exceedingly restless. She now coaxed me to let her out, and against my judgement, I did it; she had to be carried over the entry; for when I had set the gate wide open and pointed her the way into the garden, she squatted down in her usual attitude of attention, with her legs crossed, and watched me, waiting. I wanted to see how she would get through the hateful wire, so went away and hid myself, leaving her alone with Bran. I saw her creep to the entry and peer at the wire. What followed was curious. Bran came up wagging his tail and stood close to her, his side against her head; he looked down, inviting her to go out with him. Long looks passed between them, and then Bran stooped his head, she put her arms around his neck, twined her feet about his foreleg, and was carried out. Then she became a mad thing, now bird now moth; high and low, round and round, flashing about the place for all the world like a humming-bird moth, perfectly beautiful in her motions (whose ease always surprised me), and equally so in her colouring of soft grey and dusky-rose flesh. Bran grew a puppy again and whipped about after her in great circles round the meadow. But though he was famous at coursing, and has killed his hares single-handed, he was never once near Thumbeline. It was a curious sight and made me late for business.

'By degrees she got to be very bold, and taught me boldness too, and (I am ashamed to say) greater degrees of deceit. She came freely into the house and played with Florrie up and down stairs; she got on my knee at meal-times, or evenings when my wife and I were together. Fine tricks she played with me, I must own. She spilled my tea for me, broke cups and saucers, scattered my patience cards, caught poor Mary's knitting wool and rolled it about the room. The cunning little creature knew that I dared not scold her or make any kind of fuss. She used to beseech me for forgiveness occasionally when I looked very glum, and would touch my cheek to make me look at her imploring eyes, and keep me looking at her till I smiled. Then she would put her arms round my neck and pull herself up to my level and kiss me, and then nestle down in my arms and pretend to sleep. By and by, when my attention was called off her, she would pinch me, or tweak my necktie, and make me look again at her wicked eye peeping out from under my arm. 1 had to kiss her again, of course, and at last she might go to sleep in earnest. She seemed able to sleep at any hour or in any place, just like an animal.

'I had some difficulty in arranging for the night when once she had made herself free of the house. She saw no reason whatever for our being separated; but I circumvented her by nailing a strip of zinc all round the door; and I put one around Florrie's too. I pretended to my wife that it was to keep out draughts. Thumbeline was furious when she found out how she had been tricked. I think she never quite forgave me for it. Where she hid herself at night I am not sure. I think on the sitting-room sofa; but on mild mornings I used to find her outdoors, playing round Bran's kennel.

'Strap, our Fox-terrier, picked up some rat poison towards the end of April and died in the night. Thumbeline's way of taking that was very curious. It shocked me a good deal. She had never been so friendly with him as with Bran, though certainly more at ease in his company than mine. The night before he died, I remembered that she and Bran and he had been having high games in the meadow, which had ended by their all lying down together in a heap, Thumbeline's head on Bran's flank, and her legs between his. Her arm had been round Strap's neck in a most loving way. They made quite a picture for a Royal Academician; "Tired of Play" or "The End of it Romp" I can fancy he would call it. Next morning I found poor old Strap stiff and staring, and Thumbeline and Bran at their games just the same. She actually jumped over him and all about him as if he had been a lump of earth or stone. Just some such thing he was to her; she did not seem able to realize that there was the cold body of her friend. Bran just sniffed him over and left him, but Thumbeline showed no consciousness that he was there at all. I wondered, was this heartlessness of obliquity? But I have never found the answer to my question.

'Now I come to the tragical part of my story, and wish with all my heart that I could leave it out. But beyond the full confession I have made to my wife, the County Police and the newspapers, I feel that I should not shrink from any admission that may be called for of how much I have been to blame. In May, on the 13 of May, Thumbeline, Bran and our only child, Florrie, disappeared.

'It was a day, I remember well, of wonderful beauty. I had left all three of them together in the water meadow, little thinking of what was in store for us before many hours. Thumbeline had been crowning Florrie with a wreath of flowers. She had gathered cuckoo-pint and marsh marigolds and woven them together, far more deftly than any of us could have done, into a chaplet. I remember the curious winding, wandering air she had been singing (without any words, as usual) over her business, and how she touched each flower first with her lips, and then brushed it lightly across her bosom before she wove it in. She had kept her eyes on me as she did it, looking up from under her brows, as if to see whether I knew what she was about.

'I don't doubt now but that she was bewitching Florrie by this curious performance, which every flower had to undergo separately: but fool that I was, I thought nothing of it at the time, and bicycled off to Salisbury, leaving them there.

'At noon my poor wife came to me at the Bank, distracted with anxiety and fatigue. She had run most of the way, she gave me to understand. Her news was that Florrie and Bran could not be found anywhere. She said that she had gone to the gate of the meadow to call the child in, and, not seeing her, or getting any answer, she had gone down to the river at the bottom. Here she had found a few picked wild flowers but no other traces. There were no footprints in the mud, either of a child or a dog. Having spent the morning with some of the neighbours in a fruitless search, she had now come to me.

'My heart was like lead, and shame prevented me from telling her the truth, as I was sure it must be. But my own conviction of it clogged all my efforts. Of what avail could it be to inform the police or organize search-parties, knowing what I knew only too well? However, I did put Gulliver in communication with the head office in Sarum, and everything possible was done. We explored a circuit of six miles about Wilsford; every fold of the hills, every spinney, every hedgerow was thoroughly examined. But that first night of grief had broken down my shame: I told my wife the whole truth in the presence of the Reverend Richard Walsh, the congregational minister, and in spite of her absolute incredulity, and, I may add, scorn, next morning I repeated it to Chief Inspector Notcutt of Salisbury. Particulars got into the local papers by the following Saturday: and next I had to face the ordeal of the *Daily Chronicle*, *Daily News*, *Daily Graphic*, *Star* and other London journals. Most of these newspapers sent representatives to lodge in the village, many of them with photographic cameras. All this hateful notoriety I had brought upon myself, and did my best to bear like the humble, contrite Christian, which I hope I may say I have become. We found no trace of our dear one, and never have to this day. Bran, too, had completely vanished. I have not cared to keep a dog since.

'Whether my dear wife ever believed my account, I

cannot be sure. She has never reproached me for my wicked thoughtlessness, that's certain. Mr Walsh, our respected pastor, who has been so kind as to read this paper, told me more than once that he could hardly doubt it. The Salisbury police made no comments upon it one way or another. My colleagues at the Bank, out of respect for my grief and sincere repentance, treated me with a forbearance for which I can never be too grateful. I need not add that every word of this is absolutely true. I made notes of the most remarkable characteristics of the being I called Thumbeline at the time of remarking them, and those notes are still in my possession.'

WHEN AL CAPONE WAS AMBUSHED

Jack Bilbo

When he was twenty, Jack Bilbo was robbed by an American gangster on Broadway. A week or so later, down and out, he meets this same gangster again who gives him food and offers him work with 'the gangs'. Not until this German boy has been working with them for some time does he learn that he is part of Al Capone's giant organization. His story opens now, when O'Connor, one of Al Capone's lieutenants, got him enrolled as the Boss's personal bodyguard.

At eleven-thirty O'Connor came to the house, and called me. 'I have told the Boss about you,' he said. 'You are to start work as his bodyguard on trial. I hope that all will go well.'

We started off with Conny—eight of us—in two cars. On the way Conny explained my new job to me.

'The bodyguard is responsible for the safety of the Boss,' he said. 'Your job is based on the assumption that his life is always being threatened, usually by enemy gangs but sometimes by the police. We gangsters can't even trust the police these days. There are thirty-six men in the bodyguard team and eighteen of them are on duty each week. Six men, with a leader, are always on duty at his home or in his office; the watch changes every eight hours. In your spare time you can do outside "jobs" if you want to, but nothing that will bring you in danger.' He paused, then continued, emphasizing every word, 'Remember—no stranger is allowed closer to the Boss than five paces. If any one acts suspiciously, shoot him first and ask questions later.'

Conny introduced me to the man sitting next to me, a swarthy individual called 'The Captain', who looked like a Mexican. I learned later that he was from St. Louis and had been in Mexico in some bandit gang or the other. 'You keep an eye on young Sauerkraut,' Conny told him. The Captain gave me two passwords, the names of flowers, 'phlox' and 'daisy'.

As we travelled through the streets of Chicago to Capone's home I noticed that we were not bound towards one of the posh residential districts, where I had supposed Capone would live, but towards the better part of the business section. We stopped in front of a three-storey building, where no one would have expected to find a private apartment. Two small signs announced that the building contained the offices of a wholesale stocking firm and of 'Smith and Weber'. As I found later, both firms actually existed and did a regular and good business. But the stocking agency served as a weapon storage place for Capone while 'Smith and Weber' were used as a secret address.

We entered the vestibule of the building. A giant African-American operated the extraordinarily big elevator that we found there. I saw no signs of any staircase, and learned later that there was none. As the elevator moved slowly upwards the man made a telephone call from a phone in the elevator.

We arrived at the third floor and stepped out into a tiny vestibule that scarcely held the eight of us. A massive bronze door barred our way. It had neither lock nor handle on the outside, and could be opened only from within. Suddenly, without a sound, the door opened, sliding into the wall.

A man of Asian nationality and of uncertain age, dressed in dark-blue livery received us. He led us down a corridor, walking noiselessly on cork soles. I tried to imitate his quiet walk; the others tramped along noisily. As we passed through the hall I looked into one room, through the open door. It was furnished with Renaissance furniture. Then we came to a large, well-lit room at the end of the corridor, furnished likewise. Before the big window, at a huge desk, sat a man, with his back to us. I saw that his head was big, humpy, covered by thick black hair. His head was slightly drawn in between the wide shoulders and rested on a short, bull-like neck.

He rose quietly and, for his weight, lightly. He was about five-feet-seven in height. He walked towards us, smiling, taking long, sure strides. He wore a dark suit, elegantly cut, a flashy tie. He greeted all of us, shaking hands all round, first with Conny and the last one was me.

'You are the German boy?' he asked, in a deep, almost hoarse, voice.

'Yes.'

'Were you in the War?' he continued, asking the same question which Alphonso had asked.

'I was too young.'

'The Germans were good fighters,' he remarked.

Most of the pictures of Capone do not show him as he is. True, he did have a certain animal-like wildness in his face, a wildness reminiscent of a wild-cat. He carried his head erect, despite his short neck. He had strongly protruding cheek-bones, an energetic chin, hair slightly receding, black bushy eyebrows almost joined together. His eyes were small, with a very white background that offset brown pupils. His glance was piercing, strong, cunning, and perhaps a trifle sad. His nose was flat, his mouth was big, broad, thick, and his lip curved as if in scorn. His teeth were white. A scar ran down the length of his left cheek, a scar received in a fight in a Brooklyn bar-room long ago. His face had a dull dark-blue shadow from his heavy beard. He looked distinctly Italian but other blood also flowed in the veins of some of his ancestors.

After greeting us, Capone sat down at his desk and put a menthol cigarette between his lips. He began talking with Conny. The three of us were sent out to wait in another room.

This room was also furnished similarly to the others, and on close examination I found that the furniture was genuine antique. All around us were bookcases; I found later that it was Capone's library.

'We can't hear anything of what's going on in the other room,' I said to one man called 'The Count'. 'Supposing Capone wanted us?'

The Count, without a word, pointed to an alarm bell overhead.

I stepped up to the bookcases to see what Capone liked to read. The Count smiled. 'You'll find the Boss has good taste,' he said.

First I saw a big collection of erotic books. There were a lot of books which were valuable old prints. I saw a large number of books on Napoleon, some of them in expensive leather binding. *Quotes by Napoleon,* seemed to have been often read. There were thumbed-through books on every possible subject—science, business management, salesmanship, anarchism, naval warfare, architecture, grape-growing, history of the Civil War; books by Roosevelt, Ford, Mark Twain, Upton Sinclair, Stevenson, Hergeshimer, and Karl Marx. Everything was in English except for some of the French erotic literature.

I was glancing through one of the books when the door behind us suddenly opened and Capone burst into the room, livid. He waved a crumpled newspaper.

'It's enough to make you go nuts,' he said, 'when fellows like Michael Hughes use my name to gain shabby publicity for themselves. I have never seen this fellow Hughes, and he had better not let me see him. He can be fresh, but not more than that. Look at this!' He pointed to a headline:

'Hughes, police commissioner, says he has stopped work of Capone and gang in Chicago and Cook County!'

'All I can say is that if he wants to do that he'll have to get up a hell of a lot earlier,' Capone said, dropping into an arm-chair. He continued to fume. A telephone call took him back into his room.

'I wouldn't like to be in Hughes's shoes,' I said to the other two in the room.

'You wouldn't risk much at that,' said the other man, a tall blond called Andy. 'You probably don't know who made this Hughes Police Commissioner. Big Bill Thompson did it—Big Bill, the new mayor of Chicago, who is going to keep King George's snout out of American affairs, and who declared just yesterday that he was as wet and wetter than the middle of the Atlantic Ocean. And who had Big Bill elected? Who defeated Dever? The Boss!'

'That's right,' said the Count.

'Yah,' Andy continued. 'Then this louse Thompson, after the election, said that he wouldn't prosecute small alcohol cookers and bootleggers, but that he would drive "Crime and Capone" out of Chicago. That's us! Drive out those who had him elected! A lot of words—that's all, and the same with this Hughes. They just get publicity this way. We're here, and we stay here—no matter what these little newspaper fleas may write. But what makes the Boss sore is that Hughes used to be one of the best customers in Higgins's money-lending bureau. If the Boss wanted to, he could write a nice little piece about Hughes for the papers.'

'Hughes is in luck,' said the Count. 'The Boss has more to worry about now than about him.'

'Yes,' said Andy. 'There are strange gunmen in this city—Aiello's men, from St. Louis, New York, and Cleveland, who would like to get Capone. The gangster armistice is perforated like the hide of a hijacker. Competition for business is active again, and some of these strangers have even dared to turn up in the 42nd and 43rd Wards—Capone's own district! Hymie Weiss, the only one who could have hurt us, is dead. The Boss today controls all that was allotted to him by the armistice, and probably more, but new gangs with ambitions are being formed out of the remnants of the old O'Bannion crowd, and their goal is to get Capone.'

'And just think,' the Count chimed in, 'we can't ask Mr Hughes to protect us!'

'Him?' Andy asked. 'We can look out for ourselves. Hughes doesn't know anything. Wouldn't the famous Mr Hughes like to know the identity of the well-dressed man with the big diamond ring on his hand and the roll of bills in his pocket who was found dead in the Loop the other day? Ten bullets in his body. Hughes couldn't give you his name any more than he could name the man who shot him. To hell with Hughes! We've got these other mugs to look out for.'

'During the armistice not a shot was fired in Chicago for

ninety days, Sauerkraut,' the Count explained. 'Those days are over,' Andy added. 'We may have some hot times again.'

They laughed, and I laughed with them. I didn't quite understand all this, for some of the links were missing. I had to understand how all these things fitted together. Sooner than I hoped, I was to find out—in theory and in practice.

The Captain stepped into the room.

'Hurry up, boys. The Boss is going to visit "Poor Mike's." Is everything ready, German?'

In two seconds we were in the hall. Without a sound the bronze door opened. At a signal the Count and I jumped on the small platform between the door and the elevator. Immediately after us the Boss stepped out and behind him the others. Capone was laughing.

At the kerb a dark-blue sedan was waiting. Capone jumped lightly into it. The Captain put George in the front seat, beside the chauffeur, while he, Andy, and I sat in the rear with Capone. Two men, mounted on motorcycles, followed right behind us. 'You watch the left side of the road,' the Captain said curtly to me.

I sat in my place, my eyes focused on the road as we sped by, ready to shoot at the slightest sign of trouble. But there was nothing suspicious in sight. With great speed we travelled along the Lake boulevard, bound for out of town.

'Lovely weather,' said Capone suddenly.

We 'Yessed' him and continued our silent watch.

We left the city and hit the open road. On each side were trees and shrubbery. We had not gone far when *it* happened, and it happened so quickly that it is difficult to remember all the details.

I was conscious of a fast car overtaking us. As it passed the car seemed to spurt streaks of fire. The noise of shooting rose above the whirr of the motor.

At the first shot Andy and the Captain threw themselves on Capone. I also covered him instinctively. Andy had one hand free and was firing at the black car that stayed beside us. I did the same.

Suddenly George, in front, slumped in his seat, and blood spurted from his head. A moment later our chauffeur dropped over the wheel. Our car swerved, skidded, and turned over. And all this happened in about twenty seconds!

The time it took us to scramble out of our car seemed like a torturous eternity. Once out we kept shooting at the black car, now slowing down ahead of us, but we were badly covered. We made for the trees beside the road. The road which had been full of passing cars a few moments before was now desolate. A hundred feet away the black car was stopping. The two motorcycle men had not chased it, but were with us.

'Come on to the black car,' Capone ordered, taking command.

The six of us, keeping as well covered as possible, sneaked from tree to tree and from bush to bush, firing at the car as we advanced. One of the motorcycle men, Sascha, led the line. He was the first to reach the last tree before the car. He acted as a feeler, a periscope. He stuck his head out from behind the tree, but jerked it back quickly as if he did not trust the seeming lack of gun fire from the black car. Then with one step he jumped at the car. I loaded my gun for the third time. Capone, in front of me, was hurrying to the car, his face as emotionless as a steel plate.

We had nothing further to fear from the black car. We peered inside. Nothing stirred within. There lay four men in little pools of blood. We did not recognize any of them.

'These men are not gangsters,' Capone said suddenly, breaking a long silence. 'In the first place, they didn't work quickly and smoothly enough to be gangsters. Search them quickly.'

For the first time in my life I searched the pockets of a corpse. I found nothing. There was nothing to identify the men in their pockets or otherwise.

'Let's get to the hospital with our men,' Capone commanded. 'We have to get away from here immediately.'

It was dangerous for us to stay around. We found that our chauffeur was dead, so we left him in the overturned car. Sascha and George were badly wounded. I had been slightly grazed by a bullet. I carried George on my shoulder who was unconscious and weighed like a sack of lead: We had to move slowly along the road. Not a person was in sight, although the road was lined with houses. Strangely enough there was no sign of the police either.

'Where can Commissioner Hughes be?' Capone asked mockingly.

Suddenly a taxi turned from a side street into the road we were walking down. Sighting us, the car made a desperate attempt to turn and head in the other direction. We must have looked pretty wild, or perhaps the driver saw me carrying George and thought that he was dead. Andy fired a shot into the air and the taxi stopped.

The Boss went to the driver and handed him a ten-dollar bill. The Captain opened the door and we got in. We put George between Andy and myself. The taxi-driver disappeared and the Captain drove.

After ten minutes George showed some signs of consciousness. Andy pulled out a flask and poured whisky down his mouth.

Suddenly George put his hand to his head.

'Where the hell is my left ear?' he asked angrily.

It was gone—shot off.

George cursed so completely and satisfactorily that we knew he was in no serious danger.

'Better have no ears at all,' Andy said to him, 'than to have the kind you had that stick out at right angles. No wonder your left ear stopped a bullet.'

I was not too worried about George now. But Sascha was in a serious condition. I asked Andy if the hospital to which we were going was dependable, meaning whether it took good care of its patients. Andy misunderstood me.

'You bet it's dependable,' he said. 'We control it. No police can get into it.'

George seemed to have recovered, but Sascha was groaning. Andy tried to fix him up with an emergency bandage, but his pain was excruciating. The second half of our journey was covered in silence.

Capone had said nothing the whole way. Suddenly he let out one loud curse, and added, 'I know! We received threats from the Ku-Klux-Klan. It wants to rid America of me. Well, they'll have to learn to shoot better first.' After this he said no more.

The hospital was an attractive two-storey building, built in a colonial style a distance away from the road. Two nurses took charge of George and Sascha. It was in this hospital that 'Poor Mike' lay. Capone asked for the number of his room and went up to it with the Captain. We stayed downstairs and drank whisky.

In ten minutes the Boss was back. He looked gloomy and silent and none of us dared question him. We were in the car and on our way to Chicago before he said a word.

'Poor Mike is dead,' he stated simply. 'He was a good gunman.'